The Echo Mark

The Echo Mark

Gigi Carman

Contents

1

The Old King Is Gone

The fire had burned down to embers by the time William entered the chamber.

He did not speak. There was no one left to speak to. The room held only stone walls, dying light, and the absence of a man who had lived for a thousand years.

His father's body was already gone. Carried out at dawn by the King's Guard, wrapped in cloth older than most nations. There would be no burial. Vampires did not leave remains for the earth to claim. By now, the Old King had been returned to ash and wind somewhere in the mountains. A private end. The way he would have wanted it.

William stood at the window. The Scottish Highlands stretched out below, grey and green and endless. Cold air pressed against the glass. He could hear the distant call of a bird, the creak of the castle settling into itself. Nothing else.

A thousand years.

He could not imagine it. Two hundred had been long enough to watch the world shift beneath him. Long enough to bury his mother. Long enough to learn that patience was not the same as peace.

His father had believed in secrecy above all else. Hide among them. Move quietly. Do not let them see what we are. For a millennium, it had worked. Vampires slipped through human history like shadows. They built nothing permanent. They claimed nothing public. They survived by being forgotten.

But the world was changing. Technology. Cameras. Databases. The slow erosion of every dark corner. His father had seen it coming. Had worried, in his final years, that the shadows were growing thin.

Still, he had refused to step forward. Had refused to even consider it.

"Let them find us when they find us," he had said once. "Until then, we remain what we have always been. Invisible."

William exhaled. His breath fogged faintly against the window. A small reminder. He still carried heat. Still felt the echo of the human body he had once inhabited. His mother's gift to him, written into his blood before he ever understood what he would become.

She had died one hundred and forty years ago. Eighty years old, silver haired, her hand in his father's until the very end.

He had asked her once, when he was still young enough to ask such things, whether she regretted it. Loving something that would outlive her. Bearing a child who would become something she could never be.

She had smiled. Touched his face. Said only, "You were worth every minute."

His father had never been the same after she was gone. Still steady. Still present. But quieter. As if some central fire had dimmed and never returned.

William understood now. He had not understood then.

Two hundred years, and he had never found what his father had found. Never felt the pull of a matching mark. Never known if his Echo even existed somewhere in the world, born and grown and living without any knowledge of him.

That was the cost of hiding. You could not search. You could not ask. You could not reach out across the distance and say, "I am here. Are you?"

You could only wait.

His father had waited nearly eight hundred years before William's mother was born. Eight hundred years of silence. And then, against all probability, she had appeared. A human woman in a Welsh village with a mark on her shoulder that matched the one his father had carried since his own transformation.

They had fifty-five years together. A single breath in the span of his father's existence.

It had been enough. His father had said so. Had meant it.

William was not sure he believed him.

The fire popped. A log collapsed into coals. The sound was too loud in the silence.

He turned from the window.

The chamber looked the same as it always had. Stone floors worn smooth by centuries of footsteps. Tapestries too old to identify. A desk his father had used to write letters by hand long after the rest of the world had moved to screens and keyboards.

There was a letter on that desk now. Sealed with wax. William's name written across the front in his father's careful script.

He had not opened it yet.

He was not sure he was ready to hear whatever final words his father had chosen to leave behind. Advice, probably. Warnings. The accumulated wisdom of a millennium, distilled into ink and paper.

Or perhaps just goodbye.

William crossed the room. His footsteps made no sound. That was one of the first things to change, after the transformation. The body learned to move without friction. Without weight. It had taken him decades to remember how to walk like a human when he needed to.

He sat in his father's chair. The wood was cold beneath him. Everything was cold now, except in memory.

Outside, the sun was beginning to set. Orange light spilled across the mountains, catching the edges of clouds. In an hour, the world would belong to him again. He could walk the grounds without pain. Stand in the open air without flinching.

But he did not want to walk. He did not want to stand.

He wanted to sit here, in his father's chair, in his father's room, and pretend for a few more minutes that nothing had changed.

The Old King was gone.

Long live the King.

The words meant nothing. Tradition borrowed from humans who had never understood what it meant to rule for centuries instead of decades. His father had laughed at the phrase once. Said it was designed for creatures who died too quickly to learn anything useful.

William did not laugh now.

He reached for the letter. Held it in his hands. Felt the weight of the paper, the texture of the wax seal, the faint indent of his father's fingerprint pressed into the surface.

A thousand years of hiding. A thousand years of secrecy. And now it fell to him to decide what came next.

He could continue as his father had. Stay invisible. Let the world go on believing that vampires were nothing but myth and legend. Stories to frighten children. Fiction to fill books and screens.

Or he could do what his father had always refused to do. Step out of the shadows. Let them see. Let them know.

He did not know which path was right or if there was a right path at all.

But he knew he could not stay here forever. Could not sit in this chair and wait for the world to make the choice for him.

The letter remained unopened in his hands.

Outside, the last light faded from the sky.

William Stone, King of the Vampires, sat alone in the dark.

2

The Decision

The council chamber had not been used in decades.

William stood at the head of the long table and watched his advisors file in. Four of them. The last of his father's inner circle, now his by inheritance. They moved with the careful silence of old vampires, their footsteps absorbed by stone floors that had seen a thousand such gatherings.

Frederick took his seat first. He was the oldest among them, nearly seven hundred years. His face carried the stillness of someone who had stopped being surprised by anything long ago.

Beside him sat Vivian. She had served as his father's strategist for three centuries. Her eyes were sharp, assessing. She had not spoken to William directly since the Old King's death.

Samuel and Elias filled the remaining chairs. Younger by vampire standards. Only four hundred years between them. They had been born into hiding and had never known anything else.

The fire crackled in the hearth. Outside, wind pressed against the windows. The sun had set an hour ago.

William did not sit.

"Thank you for coming," he said.

Frederick inclined his head. "You are the King now. We come when called."

"My father ruled from this room for a thousand years." William looked at each of them in turn. "He believed in secrecy. In patience. But he didn't prepare for what the world would become."

No one spoke.

"For a thousand years, we have hidden. Moved through human history like ghosts. Built nothing. Claimed nothing. Survived by being invisible." He turned to face them. "My father believed this was strength. I believe it is slow extinction."

Elias shifted in his chair. "Extinction? We are immortal."

"We are not infinite." William's voice was calm. "We do not reproduce among ourselves. Our numbers grow only through transformation, which we have restricted for centuries. And finding a mate?" He paused. "How can we find them when we cannot even look?"

The silence that followed was heavy.

"The Echo Mark system exists," Frederick said carefully. "We track the births. We monitor the matches."

"In secret. Through systems humans do not know we control. Through registries they believe serve other purposes." William shook his head. "And still, how many of us have found our match? How many have waited centuries only to watch their mate live and die without ever knowing they existed?"

No one answered. They all knew the numbers. They had all lived the waiting.

"I am proposing that we end the era of shadows," William said. "Fully. Permanently. I am proposing that we reveal ourselves to the world."

The reaction was immediate.

Vivian's composure cracked. Samuel pushed back from the table. Even Frederick, ancient and unshakable, drew a sharp breath.

"You are proposing war," Vivian said.

"I am proposing survival."

"They will try to destroy us." Samuel's voice was tight with something close to fear. "Governments. Militaries. They will see us as monsters and they will act."

"Let them." William's tone did not waver. "What will they do? Shoot us? Burn us? Tear us apart with machines?" He shook his head slowly. "We are indestructible to them. Every weapon they possess, every method of execution they have devised, will fail. They will learn this quickly."

"And when they learn it?" Vivian asked. "When they realize they cannot kill us? You think that will bring peace?"

"I think it will bring reality." William moved back toward the table. "They will have two choices. Endless, futile war against something they cannot defeat. Or coexistence. Acceptance. A world where we exist openly and they learn to live beside us."

Frederick leaned forward. His ancient face was unreadable. "You speak of human choices. What of our own? There are those among us who have spent centuries perfecting invisibility. Who have built their entire existence around never being seen. They will not thank you for dragging them into the light."

"They will adapt. As they always have."

"And if they refuse?"

"Then they will learn that the world is changing whether they accept it or not." William's voice hardened slightly. "Technology. Cameras. Databases. The shadows are growing thin, Frederick. Every year, hiding becomes harder. Every year, the risk of discovery grows. My father saw it. He simply refused to act."

He placed his hands flat on the ancient wood of the table.

"We have a choice," he said. "We can wait for discovery. Let them find us on their terms, in their time, with whatever fear and panic that brings. Or we can step forward now. Controlled. Deliberate. On our terms."

Elias was shaking his head. "The risk is too great. If this goes wrong..."

"If this goes wrong, we survive." William met his eyes. "That is what we do. That is what we have always done. Humans cannot kill us. Only we can kill each other. The worst they can do is make our existence uncomfortable. And I would rather be uncomfortable in the open than comfortable in a cage of our own making."

The fire popped. Sparks rose and faded.

Vivian spoke slowly. "You have thought about this for some time."

"Since before my father died." William straightened. "He knew my views. We disagreed, but he understood my reasoning. I believe, in the end, he saw the logic. He simply could not bring himself to act on it."

"And the Echo Mark system?" Frederick asked. "The registry? If we reveal ourselves, humans will learn that we have been scanning their infants since birth. Tracking their children. Logging their marks. They will see it as surveillance. Violation."

"The Echo Mark System is hardly working, we get limited data and by the time a match is made, sometimes it's too late, we start the system again, globally, with better technology, and we make it law that every baby is scanned, not just some of them."

"You believe they will agree?"

"I believe they will have no choice but to try."

The chamber fell silent again. William could hear the wind outside, the distant settling of stone, the slow breathing of four vampires who had lived through more history than most nations.

Finally, Vivian spoke.

"If we do this," she said carefully, "there is no going back. We cannot reveal ourselves and then retreat into shadow again. The world will never unsee us."

"I know."

"And you are certain? Truly certain?"

William thought of his father. A thousand years of hiding. Eight hundred years of waiting. And in the end, only fifty-five years of happiness with a woman he had nearly missed entirely.

He thought of his own two centuries. The silence. The watching. The endless, patient hope that somewhere in the world, a mark existed that matched his own. A person he might never find because finding them meant being seen.

"I am certain," he said.

Frederick exhaled slowly. "Then we are with you. For better or worse."

Samuel and Elias exchanged glances. Then, reluctantly, they nodded.

Vivian was the last. She studied William for a long moment. Whatever she saw in his face seemed to satisfy her.

"Very well," she said. "What do you need from us?"

William felt something shift in his chest. Not relief. Something quieter. Something that felt almost like the beginning of change.

"I need you to prepare," he said. "Speeches. Logistics. Security arrangements. We will need to coordinate with human governments before any public announcement. They must not be caught entirely off guard."

"A timeline?" Frederick asked.

"One year. Perhaps less." William looked around the table. "We move carefully but we move forward. There will be no more hiding. No more waiting. When I stand before the world, I stand as something they have never seen. Something they never believed was real."

He paused.

"We begin tomorrow."

The council rose. One by one, they filed out of the chamber. Frederick lingered at the door.

"Your father would be proud," he said quietly. "And terrified."

"I know." William's voice was soft. "I am both as well."

Frederick nodded once. Then he was gone.

William stood alone in the council chamber. The fire had burned low again. The wind still pressed against the windows.

He had made his choice. There was no undoing it now.

Somewhere out in the world, humans were sleeping. Living. Breathing. Believing that vampires were nothing but stories.

William turned toward the window and watched the darkness.

Soon, he thought. Soon they would know.

And then, for the first time in a thousand years, vampires would have nowhere left to hide.

3

We Are Here

The summit had been called under false pretences.

Fourteen nations. Security Council members plus key regional powers. An emergency session regarding "a credible and unprecedented global threat." The message had been delivered through back channels, encrypted communications that governments believed were secure.

They were not secure. Nothing was secure from creatures who had watched human civilization build itself from mud and stone.

William arrived at the Geneva facility three hours before dawn. The building was nondescript. Grey concrete. No flags, no signage. The kind of place where nations discussed things they did not want the public to know.

Frederick walked beside him. Vivian followed two steps behind. They wore dark suits, modern and unremarkable. They could have been diplomats from any nation. Bankers. Lawyers. Anything but what they were.

The security checkpoint was the first test.

"Identification," the guard said. He was Swiss. Professional. Bored.

William handed over a passport. Flawless forgery. One of thousands his people had created over the centuries.

The guard scanned it. Frowned at his screen. Scanned it again.

"There's no body heat registering," he said slowly.

"There wouldn't be," William replied.

The guard looked up. Met William's eyes. Something in his face shifted. The boredom vanished, replaced by a confusion he could not name.

"Sir, I'm going to need you to step aside."

"That will not be necessary." William's voice was calm. "You will let us through. Not because I am compelling you. Simply because stopping us is not possible, and attempting to do so will only delay what must happen."

The guard's hand moved toward his sidearm.

"I would not," Frederick said quietly. "It will not help."

A long moment passed. The guard was sweating now. His instincts were screaming at him, William knew. A thousand generations of prey recognizing predator.

"Who are you?" the guard whispered.

"You will know soon enough." William stepped past him. "I suggest you remain at your post. The delegates will need calm voices when this is over."

They walked through the corridor. More guards. More checkpoints. Each one frozen by the same nameless dread. None of them tried to stop the three figures who moved like shadows through their facility.

The conference room was on the third floor. Large. Windowless. A long table surrounded by chairs, each one occupied by a representative of a nation that believed itself powerful.

William recognized some of the faces. The American Secretary of State. The British Foreign Secretary. Representatives from China, Russia, France, Germany. Others he did not know. Younger faces. Newer powers.

They looked up as he entered.

"This is a closed session," the American said. She was a sharp-featured woman with grey hair and harder eyes. "Identify yourself."

William walked to the head of the table. The chair there was empty. He did not sit.

"My name is William Stone," he said. "I am here to inform you that vampires are real. I am their king. And we are no longer willing to hide."

Silence.

Then, almost simultaneously, several delegates reached for phones. Security buttons. Panic protocols.

"Your communications have been temporarily disabled," Vivian said. She had moved to stand by the door. "They will be restored when this meeting concludes."

"This is an act of war," the Russian delegate said. He was a heavy man with a soldier's bearing. "You have infiltrated a sovereign gathering. You have made threats."

"I have made no threats." William's voice remained level. "I have stated facts. There is a difference."

"You expect us to believe you are vampires." The British delegate's voice dripped with contempt. "This is absurd. Some kind of elaborate hoax."

William considered him for a moment. Then he moved.

One instant he was at the head of the table. The next he was standing directly behind the British delegate's chair. No one had seen him cross the distance. He had simply been in one place, and then another.

The delegate scrambled to his feet, knocking his chair backward. His face had gone white.

"That is not possible," he said. "That is not..."

"And yet." William returned to the head of the table at normal speed. "I could demonstrate further, if you require. My colleague Frederick is nearly seven hundred years old. Vivian has served my family for three centuries. We have watched your nations rise and fall. We were old when your oldest institutions were young."

"What do you want?" The American's voice was steady, but her hands were gripping the table's edge. "If this is real, if any of this is real, what do you want from us?"

"To exist openly." William placed his palms flat on the table. "Nothing more. We have hidden among you for millennia. That era is ending.

Technology, surveillance, the systems you have built to monitor your own populations. They will find us eventually. All of us. We would prefer to reveal ourselves on our terms rather than be discovered on yours."

"And if we refuse?" The Chinese delegate spoke for the first time. Her voice was cool, analytical. "If we choose to treat this as a threat and respond accordingly?"

"You may try." William met her eyes. "Your weapons will not harm us. Your prisons cannot hold us. Your governments cannot destroy what they cannot kill." He paused. "But we are not here to threaten you. We are here to negotiate."

"Negotiate what?"

"Coexistence." William straightened. "We require certain things to survive. Blood, primarily. But we do not need to take it by force. Voluntary donation systems can be established. Regulated. Controlled. We are prepared to submit to reasonable oversight in exchange for legal recognition."

"You're asking us to feed you," the Russian said flatly.

"I am asking you to accept reality." William's tone hardened slightly. "We exist. We have always existed. We will continue to exist long after everyone in this room is dust. The only question is whether we exist as partners or as predators. I am offering you the former. I suggest you consider carefully before choosing the latter."

The delegates exchanged glances. Fear. Confusion. The desperate calculation of politicians confronting something outside their experience.

"There is something else," William said. "Something we will require your cooperation to build."

He nodded to Vivian. She stepped forward and placed a folder on the table. Inside were documents. Charts. Diagrams.

"Vampires do not reproduce among ourselves," William continued. "Our bonds, when they form, form with humans. There is a mark. A birthmark that appears on both the vampire and their destined mate.

Identical in shape. Identical in placement. When a match is found, we call it an Echo Mark."

The delegates stared at him. Several reached for the folder, pulling out pages.

"For centuries, we have attempted to track these marks," William said. "Informally. Imperfectly. We have gathered what data we could, when we could. But the system is failing. Matches are missed. By the time we find them, sometimes it is too late. The human has lived their entire life without knowing. Has grown old. Has died."

He let that settle.

"I am proposing we rebuild the system. Properly. Globally." William looked around the table. "Every infant scanned at birth. Every birthmark logged. A registry that spans every nation, maintained with your technology and our knowledge. When a match is confirmed, we wait. We do not make contact. We do not interfere. The human lives their life normally until they come of age."

"You want us to scan our children for you," the American said slowly. "To build you a database of potential... mates."

"I want you to help us find our other halves," William replied. "And I want you to understand what we are offering in return. Consent. Choice. Protection. When a human turns eighteen and their match is revealed, the meeting is mandatory. The bonding is not. We do not force. We do not take. Violation of these rules is punishable by death, administered by my own hand if necessary."

"Why should we believe that?" the British delegate demanded. "Why should we believe any of this?"

"Because I am telling you." William's voice was cold. "And because the alternative is that we continue as we have for millennia. Finding mates when we can. Losing them when we cannot. Growing desperate. Growing hungry." He paused. "A system benefits everyone. Structure. Rules. Accountability. Without it, there is only chaos."

The German delegate leaned forward. "You're asking us to integrate vampire... biology... into our medical systems. Our legal systems. Our entire infrastructure."

"Yes."

"The public will never accept this."

"The public will learn to accept what their governments tell them to accept." William stepped back from the table. "That is how it has always worked. That is how it will work now."

"You're very confident," the Chinese delegate said.

"I have had two hundred years to think about this moment." William met her eyes. "I am confident because I have no other choice. Neither do you."

He turned toward the door.

"You have forty-eight hours to consult with your governments. To verify what I have told you. To prepare your responses. In forty-eight hours, I will address the world directly. What I say will depend on what you decide in the time between."

"Wait." The American stood. "If we agree to negotiate. If we agree to build this registry. What guarantees do we have that you will honor any agreement?"

William paused at the threshold. He turned back to face her.

"You have my word," he said. "The word of a king who's family has ruled for two thousand years and intends to rule for two thousand more. I do not make promises lightly. And I do not break them at all."

He held her gaze for a long moment.

"Forty-eight hours," he said. "Use them wisely."

Then he was gone.

The delegates sat in silence. The folder remained on the table, its contents scattered across the polished wood. Outside, dawn was beginning to break over Geneva.

The American was the first to speak.

"Get me the President," she said. "Now."

Within the hour, secure lines were burning between fourteen capitals. Emergency sessions convened. Military advisors summoned. Intelligence agencies scrambling to verify the impossible.

Within two hours, the first leaks reached the press.

By noon, the word "vampire" was trending in every language on Earth.

And somewhere in the Swiss mountains, William Stone watched the chaos unfold and waited for humanity to make its choice.

4

The Human Answer

The first strike came seventeen hours after the summit.

William had expected it. Had told his people to expect it. Humans were creatures of fear, and fear demanded action. It did not matter that the action was futile. It only mattered that something was done.

The facility was in Nevada. Underground. The kind of place that did not appear on any map. They had taken Frederick there, along with two younger vampires who had been stationed in California.

William received the report from Vivian at dawn.

"They used incendiary rounds first," she said. Her voice was flat, clinical. "When those failed, they attempted dismemberment. Power saws. Industrial equipment."

"And?"

"He is unharmed."

William stood at the window of his temporary quarters in Geneva. The city stretched out below, grey and quiet in the early morning light. Somewhere out there, humans were waking up to a world that no longer made sense.

"The others?"

"Similar treatment. Burns. Blades. Acids." Vivian paused. "They tried drowning one of them. Held her underwater for four hours."

"She survived."

"Of course she survived. They all survived." Vivian's voice carried a note of something that might have been disgust. "The facility commander has requested additional resources. He believes more aggressive methods may yield different results."

"They will not."

"No. They will not."

William turned from the window. "And our people? How are they responding?"

"As instructed. No retaliation. No resistance. They are allowing the humans to do whatever they wish."

"Good."

"Some of them are... frustrated." Vivian chose her words carefully. "They do not understand why we permit this. They want to fight back."

"If they fight back, we become the monsters humans already believe us to be." William's voice was steady. "If we endure, we become something else. Something they cannot dismiss."

"And if they kill one of us?"

"They cannot kill us. That is the point."

The reports continued throughout the day.

In Russia, a vampire had been shot sixty-three times by a firing squad. She had stood up afterward and asked for a glass of water.

In China, three vampires had been exposed to sunlight for nine hours. They had burned. Blistered. Screamed. And when night fell, they had begun to heal.

In Brazil, a vampire had been thrown from a helicopter into the ocean. He had walked out of the surf two days later, seaweed in his hair, and politely asked for directions to the nearest phone.

Every attempt failed. Every method proved useless. And with each failure, the fear grew worse.

The public executions began on the third day.

William watched the footage from a secure location outside Zurich. They had constructed a platform in Washington. A vampire named Ruth had been brought before the crowd in chains. The executioner had used an axe.

The first blow did not sever her head. Neither did the second. By the fifth, the crowd had gone silent. By the tenth, people were screaming. Not in triumph. In horror.

The executioner stepped back, panting, his arms shaking.

The footage cut out after that. But reports said the head and body didn't even show a mark from the blows. Ruth was alive. Unharmed. Asking, again, for a glass of water.

William closed his eyes.

"Your Highness." Vivian's voice came from the doorway. "The council is asking for guidance. Some of our people want to end this. They say we have proven our point."

"We have proven nothing." William opened his eyes. "Not yet."

"They are torturing us. Publicly. For sport."

"Yes."

"And you want us to continue allowing it?"

William turned to face her. "I want us to show them what we are. Not through words. Through action. Through restraint." He paused. "Every strike they make, every failure they endure, brings them closer to the truth. We cannot be destroyed. We cannot be controlled. The only path forward is the one I offered them in Geneva."

"And if they never accept that?"

"They will." William's voice was quiet. "Because they have no other choice."

The experiments were the hardest to endure.

Not for William. He was not the one strapped to tables in underground facilities, subjected to procedures that would have killed any human a thousand times over. But the reports came daily, and each one carved a little deeper into something he had thought was already stone.

They exposed vampires to radiation, to extreme temperatures, to pressures that should have crushed diamond. They mapped every organ, every cell, every fiber of undead flesh.

And they found nothing useful. Nothing that could be weaponized. Nothing that could be exploited.

Vampires healed. Always. From everything.

On the twelfth day, William received a different kind of report.

"The American President has requested a meeting," Vivian said. "Private. No military presence. He wants to talk."

William nodded slowly. "And the others?"

"Similar requests from Britain, France, Germany. China is holding out, but their experiments have stopped. Russia..." She hesitated. "Russia is asking for terms."

"Terms."

"They want to know what we want. What it will take to end this."

William stood. Walked to the window. The sun was setting over the mountains, painting the snow in shades of gold and red.

"Tell them I will meet with all of them," he said. "Together. In Geneva. Three days from now."

"And our people? The ones still in custody?"

"They will be released. Unharmed. That is the first condition." William turned to face her. "The second is that all footage of the executions and experiments be destroyed. Every copy. Every file. What they did to us will not become a spectacle for future generations."

"They may refuse."

"They will not refuse." William's voice was cold. "They have seen what we can endure. Now they will learn what we can forgive. And they will understand that forgiveness is not the same as forgetting."

Vivian studied him for a long moment. "You planned for this. All of it."

"I hoped it would not be necessary." William moved toward the door. "But yes. I planned for it."

"And if they had succeeded? If they had found a way to kill us?"

William paused. The question hung in the air between them.

"Then I would have been wrong," he said simply. "And none of this would matter."

He left her standing in the fading light.

Three days later, the delegations began to arrive in Geneva. Their faces were different now. The contempt was gone. The disbelief was gone. What remained was something older. Something that had lived in human bones since the first of them had looked into the darkness and known that something was looking back.

Respect.

Or perhaps just the beginning of it.

William watched them file into the conference room. The same room where he had first revealed himself. The same table. The same chairs.

But everything had changed.

The American President sat down heavily. He was a tall man, grey at the temples, with the look of someone who had not slept in days.

"We're ready to talk," he said.

William nodded.

"Good," he replied. "Then let us begin."

5

Terms

The negotiations lasted nine days.

William had expected longer. Centuries of hiding, millennia of secrecy, reduced to arguments across a conference table. There were moments when he wondered if his father had been right. If hiding had been simpler. Safer. Less exhausting.

But then he remembered the experiments. The executions. The fear that had driven humans to such desperate measures.

That fear would have found them eventually. Better to face it now, on his terms, than to wait for discovery in some future decade when the shadows had grown too thin to hide in.

The American delegation led most of the discussions. Their President sat at the center of the table, flanked by advisors and military officials who watched William with barely concealed hostility.

"Blood," the President said on the second day. "That's the core issue. You need it to survive. We need to know you won't take it by force."

"We have never taken it by force on a large scale," William replied. "Individual incidents over the centuries, yes. But we are not conquerors. We are not an army. We simply exist, and we require sustenance to continue existing."

"Individual incidents." The British Prime Minister leaned forward. "You're talking about murders. Attacks. People drained and left for dead."

"I am talking about survival." William's voice remained level. "When you starve a creature, it will do what it must to live. The solution is not to moralize about the past. It is to build a future where such desperation is unnecessary."

The blood donation framework took three days to negotiate.

William proposed a system modeled on existing human blood banks. Voluntary donors. Regulated collection. Distribution managed by a joint human-vampire authority. No feeding directly from humans except in medical emergencies, and even then, only with explicit consent.

The humans pushed back. They wanted caps on how much blood vampires could receive. They wanted tracking systems. They wanted penalties for any vampire caught feeding outside the approved channels.

William agreed to all of it.

"You're being very accommodating," the Chinese Premier observed. Her tone suggested suspicion rather than gratitude.

"I am being practical." William folded his hands on the table. "We could take what we need by force. We could hunt as we did in centuries past. But that world is gone. Your cameras, your databases, your networks of information. We cannot hide forever. So instead, we build something sustainable. Something that works for both sides."

"And the Echo Mark system?" The German Chancellor had been quiet for most of the negotiations. Now she spoke with careful precision. "You mentioned it at the first summit. A registry of birthmarks. Matches between vampires and humans."

"Yes."

"You want us to scan every infant born in our countries. To build a database of our children for your benefit."

"For mutual benefit." William leaned forward. "The Echo Mark is not something we invented. It is something we discovered. A biological reality that exists whether we acknowledge it or not. When a vampire and a human are matched, there is a bond. A connection. Denying it does not make it disappear."

"What kind of bond?" The American President's voice was sharp.

"Physiological. Emotional. Difficult to describe in human terms." William paused, considering his words. "A matched pair experiences the world differently. The human is... drawn to the vampire. The vampire is calmed by the human's presence. There is recognition. Understanding. Peace."

"And if the human doesn't want to be drawn? If they reject the match?"

"Then they reject it." William's voice was firm. "The meeting is mandatory. The bonding is not. We do not force. We do not take. These rules are absolute."

"Enforced how?"

"By death." William met the President's eyes. "Any vampire who bonds with a human without consent forfeits their life. I will administer the punishment myself if necessary."

The room fell silent.

"You would kill your own people," the Russian President said slowly.

"For this, yes." William did not blink. "The bond is sacred. It cannot be built on violation. Any vampire who does not understand this does not deserve the mate they have been given."

The Echo Mark Registry took another four days.

The framework was complex. Every nation would implement neonatal scanning. Every birthmark would be logged, measured, photographed. The data would be stored in a joint database, accessible to both human authorities and vampire representatives.

When a match was confirmed, the vampire would be notified privately. They would receive only basic information: gender, country of birth, nothing more. No name. No location. No contact until the human turned eighteen.

At eighteen, the human would be informed. A meeting would be arranged. The choice would be theirs.

"What happens if they say no?" the British Prime Minister asked. "If a human refuses the bond entirely?"

"Then the vampire accepts that refusal." William's voice was quiet. "They move on. They live their existence without a mate. It has always been this way for most of us. It will continue to be this way."

"And you're certain vampires will accept this? Will follow these rules?"

"They will follow them because I command it." William stood. "And because they understand what is at stake. For a thousand years, we hid in darkness. We lost mates to time. To distance. To the simple impossibility of finding one human among billions. Now we have a chance to change that. A system. A structure. A way to find what we have been searching for."

He looked around the table.

"No vampire will jeopardize that for the sake of impatience. And those who try will answer to me."

On the ninth day, they signed the Accord.

The ceremony was simple. No cameras. No public audience. Just the leaders of fourteen nations and the King of the Vampires, gathered in a room that smelled of old paper and older stone.

William signed first. His signature was precise, unhurried. He had waited two hundred years for this moment. He could afford to take his time.

The American President signed next. Then the others, one by one, adding their names to a document that would reshape the world.

When it was done, the President looked up at William.

"This doesn't mean we trust you," he said.

"I know."

"It means we've decided you're more useful alive than dead. More manageable in the open than in the shadows."

"I understand."

"If you break this agreement. If any of your people break it." The President's voice hardened. "We'll find a way to destroy you. I don't care how long it takes."

William held his gaze.

"You are welcome to try," he said quietly. "But I suggest you spend your energy on the future instead of the past. We are part of your world now. The sooner you accept that, the easier this will be for everyone."

He turned and walked toward the door.

"One more thing." The President's voice stopped him. "The ones we held. The ones we... experimented on. Are they going to want revenge?"

William considered the question.

"I have forbidden it," he said.

"That's not what I asked."

William turned back. For a moment, something flickered in his ancient eyes. Something that might have been sympathy. Or might have been warning.

"They will do as I command," he said. "But if you want my advice? Be grateful. Be humble. And never forget what you learned in those facilities."

"What's that?"

William's voice was soft.

"That you are not at the top of the food chain. You never were. You simply did not know it until now."

He left them in silence.

The Accord was announced to the world three hours later. By morning, every newspaper on Earth carried the same headline.

The uneasy peace had begun.

6

The Registry

The first scans began six months after the Accord.

William visited a hospital in Edinburgh to observe. The building was old, Victorian brick softened by modern additions. Inside, the maternity ward hummed with the quiet chaos of new life.

He stood in the observation room, watching through glass as a technician ran a scanner over a sleeping infant. The device was small. Handheld. Designed to map every inch of skin in seconds.

"The parents consented?" he asked.

The hospital administrator nodded. She was a tall woman named Mary, grey-haired and efficient. She had not flinched when William entered the room, which he appreciated.

"All parents are informed," she said. "It's presented as a standard neonatal screening. Most don't ask questions. Those who do receive a full explanation."

"And the refusals?"

"Minimal. Less than two percent." Mary checked her clipboard. "The law requires scanning, but we've found that framing it as routine reduces resistance. People trust medical procedures they don't understand."

William watched the technician finish. The infant stirred, made a small sound, then settled back into sleep.

"No mark on this one," the technician reported. "Scan complete. Logging to registry."

The data would be uploaded within minutes. Stored in servers distributed across twelve countries. Encrypted. Protected. Accessible only to authorized personnel on both sides of the Accord.

It was not a perfect system. William knew that. Humans would find ways to resist. Some would hide their children. Others would protest, loudly, in streets and courtrooms. The scanning would become a political issue, a cultural flashpoint, a source of endless debate.

But it would continue. Because the alternative was chaos. And both sides had seen enough of that.

The vampire scans were more complicated.

They could not be done in hospitals. They required specialized facilities, secure locations where vampires could submit to examination without risk of exposure or attack. The process was slower, more personal, more fraught with centuries of accumulated privacy.

William went first.

The facility was in the Highlands, three hours from his castle. A converted estate, stone walls and modern equipment blending uneasily together. The technician was human. Young. Nervous. His hands shook slightly as he prepared the scanner.

"Your Highness," he said. "If you could remove your shirt."

William complied. The air was cold against his skin. Not that he felt it the way a human would. Temperature was a fact to him, not a sensation.

The technician began the scan. Shoulders. Back. Arms. Chest. Every inch of skin mapped and recorded, searching for the mark that might mean everything or nothing at all.

William had been scanned before. Informally. Centuries ago, when the vampires had first begun to understand the Echo Mark phenomenon. He knew what they would find.

"There." The technician's voice was hushed. "On your left shoulder blade."

William nodded. He had known it was there since his transformation. A shape like a crown, regal and precise, darker than the surrounding skin.

"Do you have a match?" the technician asked. Then he caught himself. "I'm sorry. I shouldn't have asked that."

"No," William said. "I do not have a match. Not yet."

The words hung in the air.

Not yet. As if two hundred years of waiting could be dismissed with optimism. As if the next century would be any different than the last.

He put his shirt back on and left the facility without another word.

The registry grew slowly.

Millions of human infants scanned in the first year. Tens of thousands of vampires submitting to examination. The database expanded, cross-referencing shapes and placements, searching for the impossible coincidence that meant two beings were destined for each other.

The matches were rare. Rarer than William had hoped. Rarer than anyone had expected.

In the first year, seventeen matches were confirmed. Seventeen vampires, scattered across the globe, informed that their mate had been born. Seventeen humans who would grow up not knowing what awaited them at eighteen.

Seventeen out of millions.

William read each report personally. Studied the shapes. The placements. The probability calculations that reduced love to mathematics.

He thought about his father. Eight hundred years of waiting before William's mother was born. A lifetime of patience finally rewarded for such a short time.

Was that enough? Could it ever be enough?

The council met quarterly to review the registry's progress. Frederick, Vivian, Samuel, Elias. The same faces that had been with him from the beginning.

"The system is working," Vivian reported. "Compliance rates are high. Data integrity is maintained. We have had no significant breaches."

"And the matches?" William asked.

"Forty-three confirmed in the past six months. All vampires have been notified. All are following protocol."

"No violations?"

"One attempted." Vivian's voice hardened. "A vampire in Argentina tried to locate his match before the child's eighteenth birthday. He was intercepted by local authorities and turned over to us."

"The punishment?"

"Administered. As you ordered."

William nodded. The death had been necessary. The rules existed for a reason. If even one vampire violated them, the entire system would collapse.

"The humans are asking questions," Frederick said. "About the matches. About what happens at eighteen. They want more transparency."

"Give it to them." William stood and walked to the window. "Within reason. The meeting protocols. The consent requirements. The protections we have built. Let them see that we are serious about this."

"And if they want to observe a meeting? To document the process?"

William considered. "When the first matched human comes of age, we will allow limited observation. Controlled. Supervised. They will see that we are not monsters."

"Are we not?" Samuel's voice was quiet. "Some of us have waited centuries for this. When the moment comes, when we finally meet our mate... can we trust ourselves to be gentle?"

"You can trust yourselves to obey me." William turned to face them. "The bond is sacred. I have said this before and I will say it again. Any vampire who forgets that will answer for it with their life."

The room fell silent.

"We are building something new," William said. "Something that has never existed before. A world where vampires and humans live openly. Where our bonds are recognized. Where our existence has meaning beyond mere survival." He paused. "That world requires sacrifice. Patience. Restraint. If any of you are not prepared to give those things, tell me now."

No one spoke.

"Good." William sat back down. "Then we continue."

The years passed.

The registry grew. The matches accumulated. Twenty. Fifty. A hundred. Each one a promise. Each one a future waiting to unfold.

William watched from a distance. He signed treaties. He negotiated disputes. He became a public figure, a face on screens around the world, a symbol of the uneasy peace that had settled over humanity.

The years continued to pass.

William learned to stop hoping. Hope was for creatures with short lives and shorter memories. He was neither of those things.

He had waited two hundred years. He could wait two hundred more.

Or two thousand.

Or forever.

The registry did not care about kings. It did not care about patience or longing or the quiet ache of centuries spent alone.

It simply recorded. Catalogued. Waited.

And so did William.

7

The Message

The night was quiet.

William sat in his study, reviewing trade agreements between the European vampire councils and their human counterparts. Tedious work. Necessary work. The kind of work that filled the hours between sunset and sunrise, giving shape to an existence that might otherwise dissolve into formlessness.

Rain streaked the windows. The fire had burned low. He had not bothered to add more wood. The cold did not trouble him.

A knock at the door.

"Enter," William said without looking up.

The door opened. He heard footsteps. Measured. Deliberate. The gait of someone carrying news they were not certain how to deliver.

He set down his pen.

Frederick stood in the doorway. His ancient face was unreadable, but something flickered in his eyes. Something William had not seen there in decades.

"Your Highness." Frederick's voice was careful. "A message from the Registry."

William felt nothing. He had received thousands of messages from the Registry over the years. Updates. Statistics. Reports on matched pairs and compliance rates. None of them had ever concerned him directly.

"What is it?" he asked.

Frederick stepped forward. In his hands, he held a single envelope. Cream-colored. Sealed with the mark of the Echo Registry. Standard correspondence.

Except Frederick's hands were shaking.

William looked at the envelope. Then at Frederick's face. Then back at the envelope.

"When?" he asked.

"Three hours ago." Frederick's voice was barely above a whisper. "The match was confirmed by two independent facilities. There is no error. No possibility of mistake."

William did not reach for the envelope. He sat perfectly still, his hands flat on the desk, his eyes fixed on the cream-colored paper that had suddenly become the most important object in the world.

Two hundred and twenty-seven years.

He had stopped counting. Stopped hoping. Stopped believing that this moment would ever come.

And now it was here, and he did not know what to feel.

"The details," he said. His voice sounded strange to his own ears. Distant. Detached.

Frederick opened the envelope. His eyes scanned the page.

"Female. Born six hours ago. Location: Pennsylvania, United States." He paused. "The mark is on her left shoulder. Crown shape. Identical placement to yours."

Pennsylvania. A place William had never visited. A country he had negotiated with but never truly known.

His mate had been born there. Six hours ago. A tiny human infant with a mark that matched the one he had carried for over two centuries.

"Your Highness," Frederick said. "Your mate has been born."

William closed his eyes.

He thought of his father. Eight hundred years of waiting, rewarded with fifty-five years of happiness. He thought of his mother, human and fragile and perfect, loving a monster until her last breath.

He thought of the empty centuries behind him. The routine. The duty. The endless patience that had become indistinguishable from despair.

And now this.

A child. A human child. Born into a world that had only recently learned to accept vampires. She would grow up knowing that somewhere, a creature of darkness was waiting for her. That her birthmark was not just a birthmark, but a promise.

Eighteen years. Nothing. A heartbeat. A breath.

And yet.

William opened his eyes.

"The protocols," he said. His voice was steady now. Controlled. "They remain in effect."

"Of course, Your Highness."

"No contact. No observation. No interference of any kind." William stood. Walked to the window. The rain had stopped. The clouds were breaking apart, revealing stars. "She lives her life. She grows. She becomes whoever she is meant to become. And when she turns eighteen, she will be informed."

"And then?"

William watched the stars.

"And then she will choose."

Frederick was silent for a long moment.

"You have waited over two hundred years," he said finally. "You can wait eighteen more."

"Yes." William's voice was quiet. "I can."

He stood at the window for a long time after Frederick left. The stars wheeled overhead. The night deepened. Somewhere in Pennsylvania, a human infant slept, unaware of what she was. Unaware of what she would become.

William did not know her name. Did not know her face. Did not know anything about her except that she existed, and that she was his match.

Not his to own. Not his to claim. His to wait for. His to hope for. His to meet, one day, when the world was ready.

Eighteen years.

He could endure eighteen years.

He had endured so much worse.

William turned from the window and walked back to his desk. The trade agreements still waited. The work still needed to be done. The world still turned, indifferent to the hopes of kings and the promises of birthmarks.

But something had changed.

For the first time in centuries, William Stone had something to wait for.

And for the first time in longer than he could remember, he allowed himself to feel something that might have been hope.

The night continued. The castle stood silent. And somewhere across an ocean, a child breathed her first breaths in a world that had no idea what she would mean to it.

Or to him.

8

A Mark, Nothing More

The hospital room smelled like antiseptic and exhaustion.

Clara Parker held her daughter for the first time and forgot about everything else. The fluorescent lights. The beeping monitors. The dull ache that still pulsed through her body. None of it mattered. Only this. Only her.

"She's perfect," Thomas said. His voice cracked on the word. He stood beside the bed, one hand on Clara's shoulder, the other reaching down to touch the baby's cheek. "Clara, she's perfect."

The baby made a small sound. Not quite a cry. Something softer. A question, maybe. An introduction.

"Kathryn," Clara whispered. "Her name is Kathryn."

They had chosen it months ago. A family name. Clara's grandmother had been a Kathryn. Strong and stubborn and full of love. It seemed right to carry that forward.

Thomas leaned down and kissed his wife's forehead. His eyes were wet. He didn't try to hide it.

"Welcome to the world, Katie," he said.

Outside the window, Pennsylvania stretched green under an October sky. The leaves were turning. Somewhere in the distance, a church bell rang the hour. Three o'clock in the afternoon. The exact moment their lives changed forever.

They didn't know it yet.

The technician arrived an hour later.

She was young. Efficient. She carried a small device that looked like a modified tablet, sleek and medical and utterly unremarkable.

"Standard neonatal screening," she said, smiling at Clara. "Won't take more than a minute."

Clara nodded. She had read about this. Everyone had. Since the Accord, every infant born in participating nations was scanned. Birthmarks logged. Data recorded. It was routine now. As normal as checking weight and height.

The technician unwrapped Katie gently. The baby stirred, made another of her soft sounds, then settled. The device hummed as it passed over her skin. Shoulders. Back. Arms. Legs.

"There we go," the technician murmured. She paused at Katie's left shoulder blade. Tapped something on her screen. "Small birthmark here. Crown shape. Pretty distinctive."

"Is that bad?" Thomas asked. His voice carried the particular worry of new fathers everywhere.

"Not at all." The technician smiled again. "Lots of babies have birthmarks. We just log them for the registry. Standard procedure."

Clara looked at the mark. It was small. Dark against Katie's pale skin. Shaped like a tiny crown, the edges soft but recognizable.

"Does it mean anything?" she asked.

The technician hesitated. Just for a moment. Just long enough for Clara to notice.

"It means she has a birthmark," the technician said carefully. "That's all. The chances of a match are incredibly small. Less than one in a million. Most birthmarks never echo."

Echo. The word hung in the air.

Clara knew what it meant. Everyone did now. An Echo Mark was a birthmark that matched one on a vampire. Identical shape. Identical placement. A sign that two beings were connected.

She looked down at her daughter. At the tiny crown on her shoulder.

"But it could," she said quietly. "Match, I mean. It could."

"Statistically? Almost impossible." The technician finished her scan and rewrapped Katie in her blanket. "Try not to worry about it. She's a healthy baby girl. That's what matters."

After she left, Thomas sat on the edge of the bed. He took Clara's hand.

"One in a million," he said.

"I know."

"Those are lottery odds. We've never won the lottery."

Clara managed a small laugh. "We've never played the lottery."

"Exactly." Thomas squeezed her hand. "It's just a birthmark. That's all. She's our daughter. She's going to have a normal life."

Clara looked at Katie again. The baby was sleeping now, her tiny chest rising and falling. Her face was peaceful. Untroubled.

"A normal life," Clara repeated.

She wanted to believe it. She needed to believe it.

So she did.

Six thousand miles away, night had fallen over the Scottish Highlands.

William Stone sat at his desk and read the notification for the third time. The words had not changed. They would not change, no matter how many times he looked at them.

Female. Pennsylvania, United States. Crown-shaped mark, left shoulder blade. Match confirmed.

His mate had been born.

He set the paper down carefully. His hands were steady. Two hundred and twenty-seven years of practice had taught him how to keep his hands steady even when everything inside him was not.

The fire crackled. Rain tapped against the windows. The castle was quiet around him, the way it always was in these late hours.

He should feel something. Joy, perhaps. Relief. The end of waiting.

But the waiting had not ended. It had simply changed shape. Now he waited for something else. For a child to grow. For a woman to emerge. For a choice that was not his to make.

William reached for a fresh sheet of paper. Heavy stock. Cream colored. The kind that lasted.

He didn't know what he intended to write or if she would ever read it. But the words needed to exist somewhere. Needed to be real, even if they remained unseen.

He dipped his pen in ink.

And began.

Year One

To the child who carries the echo of me,

You were born today.

I learned of it three hours ago, in a room that has not changed in two hundred years. The fire was low. The rain was falling. And a piece of paper told me that somewhere across an ocean, you had taken your first breath.

I do not know your name. I will not know it for eighteen years. I do not know your face, or the sound of your cry, or whether you have your mother's eyes or your father's nose. I know only that you exist, and that the mark on your shoulder matches the one on mine.

My mother was human. Did you know that vampires can have human mothers? I did not, until I was one. She was a Welsh woman with dark hair and a laugh that could fill a room. She lived to be eighty years old, and my father loved her every single day of those years.

I think about her often. Tonight, I think about her more than usual.

She used to say that patience was not the same as waiting. Waiting is passive, she said. Patience is active. It is choosing, every day, to trust that the future will arrive in its own time.

I am trying to be patient tonight. I am not certain I am succeeding.

These letters are foolish, perhaps. You may never read them. We may never meet. The world is uncertain, and eighteen years is a long time for humans. Anything could happen.

But I find myself wanting to mark this day. To acknowledge it somehow. To say, even if only to paper and ink, that something changed tonight.

You changed it.

Wherever you are, whoever is holding you, I hope you are warm. I hope you are loved. I hope the world is gentle with you.

That is all I have to offer. Hope, written in ink, sealed in wax, waiting in a drawer.

Perhaps that is enough.

Perhaps it will have to be.

— W

William set down his pen.

The ink dried slowly on the page. He watched it darken, watched the words become permanent.

Then he folded the letter carefully. Placed it in an envelope. Sealed it with wax, pressing his ring into the soft surface.

He did not address it. There was no address to give.

He simply wrote on the front: *Year One.*

The envelope went into a drawer. A drawer that had been empty for two hundred years. A drawer that would slowly fill with letters she might never read.

William sat back in his chair. The fire had burned low. Outside, the rain continued to fall.

Eighteen years.

He could wait eighteen years.

He had no other choice.

In Pennsylvania, Katie slept.

Clara and Thomas took turns holding her through the night. The hospital room grew quiet around them. The monitors beeped their steady rhythm. The world outside continued on, unaware that anything significant had happened.

A baby had been born. A birthmark had been logged.

Somewhere, a vampire had written a letter.

These things were connected, but the connection would remain invisible for eighteen years. For now, there was only this: a family in a hospital room, holding their daughter, dreaming of the future.

"She's going to be something special," Thomas whispered. "I can feel it."

Clara smiled. Touched Katie's cheek. Felt the warmth of new life against her fingertips.

"She already is," she said.

Outside, the October leaves continued to fall.

And the world kept turning, patient and vast, carrying them all toward a future none of them could imagine.

9

Growing Up After

Katie was five years old when she first understood that the world had changed before she was born.

The television was on. It was always on in the Parker house, humming quietly in the corner of the living room while Clara cooked dinner and Thomas read the newspaper. Background noise. White noise. The rhythm of ordinary life.

But tonight, Katie stopped playing with her blocks. She sat on the carpet and stared at the screen, where a man with pale skin and dark eyes was speaking to an interviewer.

"We have always been here," he said. "Your history is our history. We simply walked through it quietly."

Katie watched his face. His eyes. Something about him was different from other people on television, but she couldn't name what it was.

"Mama," she said. "What's a vampire?"

Clara turned from the stove. Her expression flickered. Then she smiled, warm and calm, and wiped her hands on her apron.

"They're people," Clara said. "Just a different kind of people."

"Different how?"

Clara came and sat beside her on the carpet. On the television, the interview continued, but neither of them watched it anymore.

"You know how some people have brown eyes and some people have blue eyes?" Clara asked.

Katie nodded. Her eyes were blue. Her father's were brown.

"Well, vampires are like that. They're just people who are different in some ways. They live longer. They need different things to stay healthy." Clara tucked a strand of hair behind Katie's ear. "But they're still people. They have families and jobs and homes, just like us."

"Are they scary?"

Clara was quiet for a moment.

"Some people think they're scary," Clara said finally. "But I think being scared of someone just because they're different isn't very fair. Don't you?"

Katie thought about how she felt when other kids didn't want to play with her because she was new. How it made her stomach hurt.

"That's not fair," she agreed.

"No," Clara said. "It's not."

Later, Thomas found a show about animals instead, and Katie forgot about vampires for a while. She was five. The world was full of interesting things, and most of them were closer than television.

Across the ocean, in a castle lit by firelight, William sealed his fifth letter.

The drawer was fuller now. Five envelopes, each marked with a year.

Year Five

To the child who carries the echo of me,

You are five years old today.

I have been thinking about my mother. She would have been good at this, the waiting. She had a patience I have never quite managed to replicate. When I was young and restless, she would tell me stories to settle my mind. I find myself wishing I could remember more of them.

There was one about a fisherman who waited his whole life for a particular fish. Not because the fish was valuable, but because he had seen it once, just a flash of silver in deep water, and he could not forget it. He grew old on that shore. His nets caught plenty of other fish, good fish, fish that fed his family and paid his debts. But every morning he looked toward the deep water, hoping.

I do not remember how the story ended. I think I fell asleep before she finished it. Children do that.

Five years is nothing to me. A blink. A breath. But I am aware that it is everything to you. Five years of learning to walk and talk and understand the world around you. Five years of becoming whoever you are becoming.

I hope the world has been kind to you. I hope the people around you are good. I hope you have had cause to laugh today.

These are small hopes. Perhaps too small for a king to admit to. But I have learned that small hopes are often the ones that matter most.

My mother taught me that too.

— W

The years passed the way years do for children: slowly, and then all at once.

Katie grew. She learned to read, haltingly at first, then with growing confidence. She made friends at school, lost them, made new ones. She scraped her knees and caught colds and had nightmares about monsters under her bed.

Not vampire monsters. Just regular monsters. The kind all children imagine.

She watched the world change around her, though she was too young to understand most of it. Vampires were on television sometimes. In newspapers. Her parents talked about them occasionally, in the careful way adults talked about things they didn't want children to worry about.

Katie found this mildly interesting. Not frightening. Not thrilling. Just one more piece of the puzzle that was the world.

She had other things to think about. Spelling tests. The girl who sat next to her in class and always smelled like strawberries. Whether her mother would let her stay up late on Fridays.

The mark on her shoulder was just a birthmark. Her mother had told her so. It didn't mean anything.

Katie believed her.

10

Probability

The classroom was too warm.

Katie sat near the window, watching a fly bump uselessly against the glass while Mr. Chambers wrote numbers on the whiteboard. Big numbers. The kind with so many zeros they stopped meaning anything.

"The human population," Mr. Chambers said, "is approximately eight billion people." He wrote the number out: 8,000,000,000. "The vampire population is estimated at roughly fifty thousand worldwide."

He turned to face the class.

"Now," he said, "can anyone tell me what an Echo Mark is?"

Katie was twelve. Old enough to have heard about Echo Marks, but young enough that they still felt abstract. Like learning about volcanos or black holes. Interesting, but not personal.

A few hands went up. Mr. Chambers pointed to a boy named Dylan near the front.

"It's like a soulmate thing," Dylan said. "For vampires. If a human has the same birthmark as a vampire, they're connected."

"Close," Mr. Chambers said. "But let's be more precise. An Echo Mark is a birthmark that appears on both a vampire and a human, identical in shape and placement. The match is biological, not mystical. It can be verified through scanning and comparison."

He wrote on the board: ECHO MARK = IDENTICAL SHAPE + IDENTICAL PLACEMENT.

"The registry tracks these matches," he continued. "Every infant is scanned at birth. Every birthmark is logged. When a match is confirmed, the vampire is notified, and the human is informed when they turn eighteen."

Katie shifted in her seat. Her shoulder itched suddenly. She didn't scratch it.

"Here's where the math gets interesting." Mr. Chambers wrote more numbers. "Since the registry began, approximately four hundred million babies have been scanned worldwide. Of those, roughly twelve million had birthmarks distinctive enough to be logged."

He drew a line under the numbers.

"And of those twelve million," he said, "how many do you think have been confirmed as Echo Mark matches?"

The class was silent.

"Take a guess," Mr. Chambers encouraged.

"A million?" someone offered.

"A hundred thousand?" said another.

Mr. Chambers shook his head. He wrote a number on the board.

347

"Three hundred and forty-seven," he said. "In over twenty years of scanning. That's the total number of confirmed Echo Mark matches."

The room went quiet. Katie stared at the number.

"Less than one in a million," Mr. Chambers said. "That's your odds of being an Echo Mark match. You're more likely to be struck by lightning twice."

A girl near the back raised her hand. "But it does happen, right? There are matches?"

"Yes. It happens." Mr. Chambers leaned against his desk. "And when it happens, it's significant. Echo Mark pairs are formally recognized. They have legal protections. The vampire community considers them sacred."

"What happens at the meeting?" Dylan asked. "When someone turns eighteen?"

"The meeting is mandatory. Attendance is required by law. But the bonding is not. The human hears who their match is, they have a conversation, and then they decide whether to continue the relationship." Mr. Chambers paused. "They can say no. They can walk away. That choice is always theirs."

Katie filed this information away the same way she filed away everything else she learned in school. Interesting. Unlikely to ever matter.

The odds were clear.

That night, Katie asked her mother about the Echo Mark.

They were doing dishes together, the way they always did. Clara washed, Katie dried. The rhythm was familiar, comforting.

"We learned about it in school today," Katie said. "The probability."

Clara's hands paused in the soapy water. Just for a moment. Then she continued scrubbing.

"What did they teach you?" she asked.

"That it almost never happens. Less than one in a million." Katie dried a plate slowly. "Is that why you never talked about my birthmark? Because the odds are so low?"

"We never wanted you to worry about something that would probably never matter," Clara said. "You have a birthmark. So do lots of people. The chances of it meaning anything are almost zero."

"Almost zero isn't zero."

"No." Clara turned to look at her. "It's not. But Katie, you can't live your life waiting for something that probably won't happen. You live your life, and then you deal with things if they come."

Katie nodded. That made sense.

"I don't think it'll happen," she said. "The math says it won't."

"The math probably says it won't," Clara agreed.

Katie finished drying the dishes and went to do her homework. She didn't think about the birthmark again for a long time.

In Scotland, William added another letter to the drawer.

Year Twelve

To the child who carries the echo of me,

This month I learned that a girl died.

She was fourteen. Her name does not matter here. I did not know her. I never would have known her. She was human, and she carried an Echo Mark that matched a vampire who had waited four hundred years to meet her.

The match was perfect. The shape. The placement. Everything we look for when we dare to hope.

She was killed in an accident. A car on a wet road. Nothing dramatic. Nothing that would make history. Just a moment of inattention, and a life ended before it had properly begun.

I am told the vampire asked if the meeting rules could be bent. Just this once. He wanted to see her face. To say her name. To know something, anything, about the person he had waited for.

I told him no.

I did not do it lightly. Rules are easy to defend in theory. Much harder when they stand between someone and their grief. But the rules exist for a reason. Waiting protects choice. Breaking it would not have saved her. It would only have changed the shape of the loss.

Still, tonight I am reminded that waiting is not without risk. That time does not pause simply because we ask it to. That the future we imagine is never guaranteed.

I do not write this to frighten you. I write it to remind myself that patience is not safe. It is simply necessary.

If you are reading this someday, it will mean that you survived the years I could not protect you from. That the ordinary dangers of the world did not take you before you had the chance to choose your own path.

That knowledge brings me more comfort than you might expect.

Wherever you are tonight, I hope you are alive. I hope you are laughing at something small and unimportant. I hope the world has not asked too much of you yet.

— W

Katie found the book by accident.

She was twelve, browsing the school library during lunch because the cafeteria was too loud and her usual table had been taken over by a group of eighth graders. The library was quiet. Empty, mostly. The librarian barely looked up when she came in.

She wandered through the stacks without purpose, running her fingers along spines, reading titles without really seeing them. History. Science. Fiction. More history.

And then, tucked between a book about the Civil War and one about ancient Rome, a slim volume with a plain cover: *The Stone Interviews: A Complete Record.*

Katie pulled it out. The cover was unremarkable. Just text on a dark background. Inside, she found transcripts. Questions and answers, laid out plainly, without commentary.

She sat down at a table near the window and began to read.

The interviews were old. Conducted years ago, when the Accord was still new. But the questions were the kind she had wondered about herself.

INTERVIEWER: Why hide? For so long, why hide?

STONE: Survival. It is simpler than it sounds. We are few, and you are many. Your greatest strength has always been your numbers. Your ability to coordinate. To build systems that multiply your power.

INTERVIEWER: But you could have conquered us.

STONE: Perhaps. For a time. And then what? We cannot reproduce among ourselves. Our numbers grow slowly. And we need you. Not just for blood. For everything.

INTERVIEWER: Everything?

STONE: You create things. Art. Music. Ideas. You change so quickly, generation after generation, reinventing yourselves constantly. We watch and we learn and we are shaped by what you make. Without you, we would stagnate. We would become fossils. Powerful, perhaps, but purposeless.

Katie paused at that. Fossils. She had never thought of vampires that way. As creatures who could become stuck. Who needed humans to keep them moving.

She kept reading.

INTERVIEWER: The Echo Mark. You believe it's biological?

STONE: It is demonstrably biological. The match can be verified through medical imaging.

INTERVIEWER: And when a match is found?

STONE: We are notified. Told only that the match exists. Nothing more.

INTERVIEWER: That must be difficult. Knowing but not knowing.

STONE: It is what it is. The waiting is not the hard part. The hard part is the uncertainty. Whether the person will want to know you. Whether the connection will mean anything to them.

INTERVIEWER: And if they don't? Want to know you?

STONE: Then we accept it. There is no other choice.

Katie closed the book. Her chest felt strange. Tight in a way she couldn't explain.

11

Hard Years

The summer Katie turned thirteen, her father lost his job.

He didn't tell her at first. She figured it out from the silences. The way her parents talked in low voices after she went to bed. The way her mother started clipping coupons again.

"Dad's looking for new work," Clara said finally, one evening in July. "It might take a while. We need to be careful with money."

Katie nodded. She understood careful with money. They had always been careful with money. This was just more careful.

"Can I help?" she asked.

Clara smiled. Touched her cheek. "You can help by being you. That's enough."

Katie tried to believe that. She was not very successful.

The changes came slowly. Little things at first. No more trips to the mall with friends. No more new books, the library would have to do. No more pizza Fridays.

Katie didn't complain. She could see how hard her parents were trying. Complaining would only make it worse.

Her friend Rachel noticed anyway.

"You never want to do anything anymore," Rachel said one afternoon at school.

"I'm busy," Katie said. It was easier than explaining.

"With what?"

Katie shrugged. She didn't know how to say that busy meant worried. That busy meant listening for her parents' voices through the wall at night, counting the sighs, measuring the silences.

They drifted apart after that. Not dramatically. Just quietly. The way friendships sometimes end when you're thirteen and everything feels fragile.

Thomas found work in October. Not his old job. Something different. Longer hours, less pay. But it was work.

"We're going to be okay," Clara said that night at dinner. Her eyes were wet but her smile was real. "We're going to be just fine."

Katie nodded. She filed this away: okay was fragile. Fine was temporary. The ground could shift without warning.

She started paying attention to money. Not obsessively. Just practically. Noticing prices. Saving small amounts when she could.

"You don't have to do that," Thomas said when he saw her counting coins.

"I want to," Katie said. "Just in case."

Thomas was quiet. Then he sat down beside her.

"I'm sorry," he said. "That you had to learn this so young."

"Learn what?"

"That the world isn't always safe. That sometimes things fall apart." He put his arm around her. "I wanted to protect you from that."

Katie leaned into him. He smelled like sawdust and coffee.

"It's okay, Dad. I'm okay."

"You're more than okay." His voice was rough. "You're the best thing I've ever done."

They sat together for a while. Outside, the October wind rattled the windows. The world felt small and contained. Safe enough.

Whatever happened, she had this. She had them.

That was enough.

Year Thirteen
To the child who carries the echo of me,

You are thirteen today.

Thirteen years is a strange measure of time. Long enough for the world to change its mind about things it once feared. Not long enough for it to understand them.

When we first stepped into the open, humans spoke as if everything had to be decided immediately. Who we were. What we would become to one another. Whether coexistence was possible. Now, years later, the urgency has softened. People adapt. They always do.

I find myself watching that adaptation more closely than I expected. The way fear becomes habit. The way habit becomes background. The way something extraordinary can fade into normality without anyone quite noticing when it happened.

I wonder sometimes if this is how growing up works. Not in moments, but in gradual shifts you only recognise after they have already passed.

I do not know where you are in your life as I write this. I only know where the world is. It is steadier now. Quieter. Less inclined to panic. That feels important. It feels like progress.

There will come a day when questions that have been theoretical for years begin to feel more immediate. I am not afraid of that day. I am simply aware of it. Awareness is something I have learned to value.

Until then, I remain where I have always been. Watching. Waiting. Allowing time to do what it does best.

I hope the world you are growing into is gentler than the one I inherited.

— W

Katie was fifteen when she stopped thinking of vampires as unusual.

It happened gradually. The way you stop noticing a painting that hangs in your living room, or the sound of traffic outside your window. Vampires were just there. Part of the background. Mentioned in news broadcasts and referenced in textbooks and occasionally interviewed on late-night television.

She watched one of those interviews with her parents one evening. A vampire couple, one of the rare Echo Mark pairs, promoting a book about their experience.

"It's normal," the human woman was saying. "That's what people don't understand. It's just normal."

"But he's three hundred years old," the host pressed.

"At first, maybe that was strange. But you adapt." The woman took the vampire's hand. "He's just Henry to me. My husband. The guy who forgets to put the milk back in the fridge."

The audience laughed. Katie watched the vampire smile. It was careful, controlled, but something genuine flickered beneath it.

"I have lived through seventeen wars," he said. "But I cannot remember where we keep the coffee mugs."

More laughter.

Katie found herself smiling too. Not because it was funny, exactly. Because it was human. Or close enough to human that the difference stopped mattering.

After the interview ended, she thought about it for a while. About what it would mean to love someone who would outlive you by centuries. Who would watch you grow old while they stayed the same.

It seemed difficult. But the couple on television hadn't seemed unhappy. They had seemed content. Comfortable with each other in the way married people sometimes were.

Maybe that was enough. Maybe love didn't require everything to make sense.

Year Fifteen

To the child who carries the echo of me,

You are fifteen today. Three more years.

I watched an interview recently. A matched pair, speaking about their lives together. They seemed happy. Genuinely happy. The kind of happiness that comes from understanding rather than passion.

My parents had that. Understanding. My mother used to say that passion was easy. Anyone could feel passion. But understanding required work. It required listening, and learning, and accepting the parts of someone that did not fit neatly into what you expected.

She understood my father in ways I still do not fully grasp. She knew when he needed silence and when he needed distraction. She knew how to make him laugh, which was rare and difficult. She knew how to pull him back from the dark places his mind sometimes went, the places where centuries of memory became a weight rather than a gift.

He understood her too. Her stubbornness. Her fierce pride. Her refusal to be diminished by anyone, including a king. He loved her not despite these things but because of them.

I have wondered, often, whether I am capable of that kind of understanding. Whether two hundred years of solitude have made me too set in my ways. Too accustomed to my own thoughts, my own rhythms, my own silent rooms.

I do not know. I suspect I will not know until I am tested.

Three more years. The drawer is almost full. The waiting continues.

I hope you are happy. I hope, more than anything, that you are becoming someone you are proud to be.

— W

12

Almost

Katie turned seventeen on a Tuesday.

There was no party. She hadn't wanted one. Just dinner at home, her mother's pot roast, a cake from the bakery downtown. Small and quiet and exactly right.

Her mother gave her a bracelet that had belonged to her grandmother. Silver, delicate, old-fashioned.

"She would have loved you," Clara said. "She really would have."

Katie didn't remember her grandmother. But she had heard stories. A strong woman. Stubborn. Full of opinions.

"One more year," Clara said, clasping the bracelet around Katie's wrist. "Then you're an adult."

"Legally," Katie said. "I don't feel like an adult."

"No one does. That's the secret." Clara smiled. "You just get older and hope no one notices you're still figuring it out."

Katie laughed. She looked at the bracelet, turning her wrist to catch the light.

One more year.

The thought felt strange. Abstract. Eighteen had always been distant, theoretical. A someday kind of thing. Now it was soon.

"Then what?" Katie asked.

"Then whatever you want." Clara tucked a strand of hair behind Katie's ear. "College, if you can swing it. Work, if you can't. Your own life. Your own choices."

"That sounds scary."

"It is scary. But it's also exciting." Clara smiled. "You're going to be fine, Katie. Better than fine."

Katie wanted to believe it. She tried to believe it.

The guidance counselor called her in the following week.

Mrs. Turner was a tired woman with kind eyes and too many students to keep track of. She shuffled papers as Katie sat down.

"Kathryn Parker. How are you doing?"

"Fine," Katie said. "Is something wrong?"

"No, nothing wrong. Just checking in. You're seventeen now. Senior year is coming. We need to start thinking about next steps."

Katie nodded. They talked about community college. Scholarships. Realistic plans for realistic futures.

And then Mrs. Turner paused.

"One other thing," she said. "You're flagged in the system."

Katie's stomach tightened. "Flagged?"

"For the Echo Mark registry. You have a logged birthmark." Mrs. Turner's voice was matter-of-fact. "When you turn eighteen, you'll receive an official notification. If there's no match, which is almost always the case, you get a letter confirming that. If there is a match, you'll be contacted about the mandatory meeting."

Katie knew all this. She had learned it in school years ago.

But hearing it in an office, from an official, made it feel different. More real.

"The odds are almost zero," Mrs. Turner added. "I just wanted you to be prepared."

"Prepared for what?"

"For eighteen. It's a big birthday for everyone with a logged mark."

Katie nodded. She walked out of the office on legs that felt strange.

She didn't tell her parents about the conversation. There was nothing to tell. The odds were the same as they had always been.

Almost zero.

Almost zero wasn't zero.

But it was close enough.

Year Seventeen

To the child who carries the echo of me,

You are seventeen today. One more year.

I find myself uncertain what to write. Everything I have said before feels insufficient. Everything I might say next feels premature.

I have lived for two hundred and forty-four years. I have ruled for decades. I have negotiated with nations and shaped treaties that will outlast everyone currently alive. And I do not know what to say to someone I have never met.

Perhaps that is honest, at least. Perhaps honesty is all I have left to offer.

I am afraid.

There. I have written it. A king, afraid. Afraid of a meeting that may go badly. Afraid of hope that may prove unfounded. Afraid of finding, after all this waiting, that the connection means nothing. That the mark is biology without meaning. That I have spent eighteen years writing letters to someone who will look at me and feel only the obligation of law.

Fear is not dignified. It is not royal. But it is true.

I do not know who you are. I do not know who you are becoming. I know only that one year from now, we will sit across from each other, and you will decide whether I am worth knowing further.

I have prepared myself for rejection. I have rehearsed acceptance. I have told myself, again and again, that your choice is yours alone, and that I will respect it without complaint.

I am not certain I believe myself.

But I will try. That is all I can promise. That I will try to be worthy of whatever you decide.

One more year. The drawer is nearly full.

I hope you are ready. I am not sure I am.

— W

13

Eighteen

Katie woke to the smell of pancakes.

For a moment, she lay in bed with her eyes closed, listening to the sounds of the house. Her mother moving in the kitchen. Her father's voice, low and warm, saying something she couldn't quite make out. The clatter of dishes. The sizzle of batter hitting a hot pan.

Eighteen.

She was eighteen years old today.

The thought felt strange. Like wearing clothes that didn't quite fit. She had been seventeen for so long that eighteen seemed like a costume she wasn't sure she deserved.

She opened her eyes. Sunlight streamed through her curtains, warm and golden. October light. Her favourite kind.

"Katie!" Her mother's voice floated up the stairs. "Breakfast is ready!"

Katie stretched. Got out of bed. Looked at herself in the mirror above her dresser.

The same face she had always had. Brown hair that never did what she wanted. Blue eyes that were, according to her mother, exactly like her grandmother's. A nose she had inherited from her father, slightly too long. A mouth that smiled easier than it frowned.

Eighteen years of this face. Eighteen years of this body. Eighteen years of being Kathryn Parker from rural Pennsylvania, daughter of Clara and Thomas, student of middling grades, dreamer of small dreams.

She didn't feel different.

But she was, now. Legally. Officially.

An adult.

Breakfast was pancakes and bacon and eggs. Her father made coffee, even though Katie didn't usually drink it. Her mother had put candles on the pancakes, which was silly, but Katie blew them out anyway.

"Make a wish," Clara said.

Katie closed her eyes. She didn't know what to wish for. She never did. Wishes felt presumptuous. Like asking the universe for things you hadn't earned.

She wished for things to stay the same. For her parents to be healthy. For the house to stay warm in winter. For the small, ordinary happiness she had built to remain intact.

She blew out the candles.

"Happy birthday, sweetheart." Thomas raised his coffee cup. "To our daughter. The best thing we ever did."

"Dad." Katie felt her face flush.

"It's true." Clara reached over and squeezed her hand. "We are so proud of you, Katie. So proud of who you've become."

Katie didn't know what to say. She ate her pancakes instead. They were perfect. Fluffy, with just the right amount of syrup. Her mother always made them perfect.

After breakfast, there were presents. Small things. A new sweater Clara had saved for months to afford. A book Thomas had found at a yard sale, something about history that Katie had mentioned wanting. A card with money tucked inside, less than last year, but Katie pretended not to notice.

"Thank you," she said. "Really. Thank you."

"There's one more thing." Clara stood up. "Wait here."

She disappeared into the kitchen and came back with a box. It was small. Wrapped in silver paper. Old paper, Katie realized. Saved from some previous occasion.

"This was going to be for graduation," Clara said. "But I decided you should have it now."

Katie unwrapped the box carefully. Inside was a pendant on a thin silver chain. Small. Delicate. Shaped like a crown.

She stared at it.

"It was my mother's," Clara said. "She wore it every day. When she died, I put it away. I was waiting for the right time to give it to you."

Katie touched the crown shape. It was cool against her fingers. Almost exactly the size of the mark on her shoulder.

"Mom," she whispered.

Katie stood up and hugged her mother. She didn't have words. The pendant felt heavy in her hand, heavier than something so small should be.

"I love it," she said. "I love you."

"I love you too, sweetheart." Clara held her tight. "Happy birthday."

The day passed quietly.

Katie did homework. Read her new book. Helped her mother with dinner. Ordinary things. Comfortable things. The rhythm of a life she knew by heart.

But something was different. She felt it in the back of her mind, like a door left slightly open. A draft she couldn't locate.

Today was her eighteenth birthday. The day when everything was supposed to become clear. The day when, if her mark had matched, she would be notified.

The odds were against her. She knew that. One in a million. Less than one in a million.

But the day felt heavy anyway. Like the air before a storm.

She didn't say anything to her parents. There was nothing to say. Either something would happen or it wouldn't. Worrying wouldn't change the outcome.

Dinner was pot roast. Katie's favorite. They ate in the dining room instead of the kitchen, which they only did on special occasions. Clara had put out the good dishes. The ones with the tiny flowers around the edges.

"To Katie," Thomas said, raising his glass. "Eighteen years of joy. Eighteen years of love. And many, many more to come."

They clinked glasses. Katie smiled. The food was good. The company was better.

For a little while, she forgot about the mark. Forgot about the registry. Forgot about everything except this moment, this table, these people who loved her.

The knock came at seven o'clock.

Katie was in the living room, curled up on the couch with her book. Her parents were in the kitchen, washing dishes together the way they always did. The house was warm. The evening was quiet.

And then, a knock.

Three sharp raps on the front door.

Katie looked up. Her parents had stopped talking in the kitchen. She could feel the silence spreading through the house like cold water.

"I'll get it," Thomas said.

Katie heard his footsteps in the hall. Heard the door open. Heard a voice she didn't recognize. Low. Official.

"Mr. Parker?"

"Yes?"

"My name is Samuel Ward. I'm here on behalf of the Echo Mark Registry."

Katie's book fell from her hands.

She stood up. Her legs felt strange beneath her. Too light. Too loose. Like they might stop working at any moment.

She walked to the hallway.

Her father stood in the doorway. Behind him, she could see a figure on the porch. A man in a dark suit. Pale skin. Still face.

A vampire.

"There must be a mistake," Thomas was saying. "The odds are—"

"There is no mistake, Mr. Parker." The vampire's voice was calm. Patient. "The match was confirmed at birth. We have waited eighteen years to make contact. Your daughter, Kathryn Parker, has been identified as having an Echo Mark."

Katie stopped breathing.

The world tilted. The walls seemed to contract. Everything she had believed about her life, about her future, about who she was and who she would become, crumbled in the space of a single sentence.

Her mother appeared beside her. Took her hand. Squeezed.

"Katie," Clara whispered. "Katie, breathe."

Katie breathed. The air felt thin. Wrong.

"Who?" she heard herself ask. Her voice sounded far away. Like someone else speaking with her mouth. "Who is the match?"

The vampire on the porch paused. His expression flickered with something Katie couldn't read.

"Your match," he said, "is His Majesty, King William Stone. You have been summoned to attend the mandatory meeting. Transportation has been arranged."

The world went white around the edges.

Clara's hand tightened on hers.

Thomas said something, his voice rising, but Katie couldn't hear the words.

She could only hear one thing. One phrase. Playing over and over in her mind.

King William Stone.

The vampire king.

Her match.

In Scotland, William stood at the window of his study.

The fire had burned down to embers. The night was cold and clear. Stars scattered across the sky like salt on black velvet.

He had received the notification three hours ago. The meeting was set. Transportation arranged. Everything in motion.

Eighteen years.

The waiting was over.

Two days, he would see her face for the first time. Hear her voice. Learn whether the hope he had carried for so long had any foundation at all.

He looked at the drawer where the letters waited. Eighteen envelopes. Eighteen years of words.

He had not written one for today. There was nothing left to say. Nothing that words could capture.

Only waiting.

Only hope.

Only the quiet, terrifying knowledge that everything was about to change.

William turned from the window and walked into the darkness.

The future was coming.

Ready or not.

14

The Journey

Katie did not sleep.

She lay in her bed and watched the ceiling and listened to the house settle around her. The same creaks she had heard every night for eighteen years. The same rhythm of her parents moving through the rooms below. The same quiet.

Except nothing was the same.

The messenger had left hours ago. Samuel Ward. That was his name. He had handed her parents a folder of documents and explained the timeline in a voice that expected no argument. Transportation would arrive at nine in the morning. A car to the airport. A private flight. Arrival in Scotland by evening.

Scotland.

Katie had never left Pennsylvania. She had barely left her county. And now she was supposed to fly across an ocean to meet a king.

A vampire king.

Her match.

She turned onto her side. Through her window, she could see the black SUVs still parked on the street. Security, Samuel had called them. Protection during the transition period. They would remain until she left.

Protection from what? She did not ask. She was not sure she wanted to know.

Downstairs, her parents' voices rose and fell. Too quiet to hear the words. Too tense to mistake for ordinary conversation.

Katie closed her eyes. She did not sleep.

Morning came grey and cold.

Katie showered. Dressed. Looked at herself in the mirror and did not recognise what she saw.

The same face. The same body. But something behind her eyes had shifted. Something that understood, finally, that ordinary was over.

Her mother had packed a suitcase. Katie did not remember asking her to. She found it by the front door when she came downstairs, neatly organised, everything she might need for a month away from home.

A month.

That was the timeline. Samuel had explained it last night. One month of courtship. One month to decide whether she wanted to proceed with the bond. One month to determine if the match meant anything beyond biology.

"You don't have to do this," Thomas said.

He was standing in the kitchen doorway. He looked like he had not slept either. His eyes were red. His shoulders were tight.

"I think I do," Katie said.

"The meeting is mandatory. The rest of it isn't." His voice was rough. "You can walk away. After the meeting. You can come home."

"I know."

"Do you?" Thomas crossed to her. Took her hands. His grip was too tight. "Katie, this is the vampire king. The most powerful creature on the planet. If you go there, if you stay, I don't know how to protect you."

"Dad." Katie squeezed his hands back. "I don't think I need protection. Not from him."

"You don't know that."

"No. But the rules exist for a reason. He built them himself." She had read about it. Years ago. The interviews. The treaties. The careful structure that governed Echo Mark meetings. "He won't hurt me."

Thomas stared at her. His jaw worked.

"And if you're wrong?"

Katie did not have an answer for that.

The car arrived at nine exactly.

Not a car. An SUV. Black, sleek, windows so dark she could not see inside. A driver in a suit stepped out and opened the rear door. He did not smile. He did not speak. He simply waited.

Katie looked back at the house. The porch where she had spent summer evenings reading. The window of her bedroom. The mailbox her father repainted every spring.

She had not said goodbye to any of it. She had not known she needed to.

"Ready?" Clara's voice was steady. Too steady. The kind of steady that took effort.

"No," Katie said. "But I don't think that matters."

They climbed into the SUV. The interior was leather. Cool and clean. More space than Katie had expected. Her parents sat on either side of her, close enough that she could feel their warmth.

The driver closed the door. The world outside disappeared behind tinted glass.

The SUV pulled away from the curb.

Katie watched her street slide past. The neighbours' houses. The park where she had played as a child. The convenience store where she bought candy after school.

All of it familiar. All of it fading.

She did not look back.

The airport was not what she expected.

They did not go to the terminal. The SUV turned onto a service road, passed through a security gate, and drove directly onto the tarmac.

A plane waited there. Small. White. Gleaming in the morning light.

Private, Katie realised. Of course it was private. She was going to meet a king.

The driver opened the door. Cold air rushed in, sharp with the smell of jet fuel. Katie climbed out on legs that felt unsteady.

"This way, Miss Parker."

A woman in a dark suit stood at the base of the aircraft stairs. Human, Katie thought. Something about the way she moved. The warmth in her cheeks.

"Your luggage will be loaded. Please board when ready."

Katie looked at her parents. Clara's face was pale. Thomas's jaw was clenched so tight she could see the muscles jumping.

"We're all going," Clara said. It was not a question.

"Yes, ma'am. Accommodations have been prepared for your family."

They climbed the stairs together. Katie first. Her parents behind. Each step felt heavier than the last.

The interior of the plane was quiet luxury. Leather seats. Soft lighting. A small table with water and fruit. Everything restrained. Nothing excessive.

An attendant appeared. Young. Human. Professional.

"Welcome aboard. Flight time to Edinburgh is approximately eight hours. Please let us know if you need anything."

Eight hours.

Katie sank into a seat by the window. Watched the ground crew moving around the plane. Felt the vibration as the engines started.

This was happening. This was real.

Her mother took the seat beside her. Reached over and took her hand.

"We're with you," Clara said quietly. "Whatever happens. We're with you."

Katie nodded. She did not trust her voice.

The plane began to move.

The clouds were endless.

Katie watched them for hours. White and grey and stretching to the horizon. The world below invisible. The world above empty.

She tried to imagine the king. William Stone. She had seen photographs, of course. Everyone had. The interviews. The broadcasts. The formal portraits that appeared in textbooks and news articles.

Dark hair. Pale skin. Eyes that seemed to look through the camera rather than at it. Handsome, in the way that statues were handsome. Perfect and remote.

Two hundred years old. Maybe more. She could not remember the exact number.

He had been waiting for her since she was born. Eighteen years of knowing she existed without knowing who she was. Eighteen years of patience.

What did that kind of patience do to a person?

She was not sure she could imagine it.

Her father slept. Her mother read a book without turning the pages. The attendants moved quietly, offering food and drinks that no one wanted.

Katie watched the clouds and tried not to think about what waited on the other side.

The descent was gentle.

Katie felt the pressure change in her ears. Watched the clouds thin and break apart. And then, suddenly, land. Green and grey and stretching to the horizon.

Scotland.

It looked like the photographs. Rolling hills. Dark patches of forest. Stone walls cutting across fields like stitches in fabric. A different kind of beautiful than Pennsylvania. Older. Wilder.

The plane touched down smoothly. Taxied to a stop. The engines wound down into silence.

"Miss Parker." The attendant appeared at her elbow. "We've arrived. Your transport is waiting."

Katie unbuckled her seatbelt. Stood on legs that had forgotten how to work properly. Walked to the door of the plane.

The air hit her first. Cold. Clean. Smelling of rain and something green she could not name.

Two cars waited on the tarmac. Black. Long. The kind of cars that carried important people to important places.

Katie was not important. She was a girl from rural Pennsylvania who had never been anywhere.

But her mark was important. And that, apparently, was enough.

They drove for over an hour.

The landscape changed as they went. Cities gave way to towns. Towns gave way to villages. Villages gave way to nothing but hills and sky.

Katie pressed her face to the window. Watched the light fade from gold to grey. Watched the first stars appear in the darkening sky.

And then she saw it.

The castle.

It rose from a hillside in the distance. Stone walls. Towers. Windows catching the last light of sunset. Not gothic, not dramatic. Just solid. Ancient. A building that had watched centuries pass and expected to watch centuries more.

Katie's breath caught.

This was where he lived. Where he had lived for longer than her country had existed.

This was where she would stay for the next month. Where she would learn whether the mark on her shoulder meant anything at all.

The car wound up a long drive. Through gates that opened automatically. Past gardens that were shadows in the failing light. Up to a door that was older than anything Katie had ever touched.

The car stopped.

A man in a dark suit opened her door. The cold rushed in again.

"Welcome to Castle Stone, Miss Parker. I am Frederick. I will show you to your quarters."

Frederick. Katie remembered the name from somewhere. The king's advisor. One of the oldest vampires in the court.

He looked like a man in his fifties. Distinguished. Calm. His eyes held something ancient and patient.

"Thank you," Katie managed.

"Your family will be housed in the east wing. Private quarters. All amenities provided." Frederick gestured toward the door. "Please, follow me."

They walked through halls that seemed to go on forever. Stone floors. Tapestries. Paintings that Katie did not have time to examine. The castle was warm inside, heated by means she could not see.

It felt lived in. That was what surprised her most. Not a museum. Not a monument. A home.

An old home, vast and strange. But a home nonetheless.

Frederick stopped before a heavy wooden door.

"The family wing," he said. "Three rooms have been prepared. Yours is at the end of the hall. Your parents will be nearby."

He opened the door. Katie stepped through.

The sitting room was comfortable. Sofas. Armchairs. A fireplace already lit. Bookshelves lining one wall. Windows that looked out over darkness.

"You have two hours before the formal meeting," Frederick said. "Time to rest. To change. To prepare yourself."

"The meeting," Katie repeated. Her voice sounded far away.

"With His Majesty." Frederick's expression did not change. "He is aware of your arrival. He will not approach until you are ready."

Katie nodded. She did not know what else to do.

Frederick inclined his head slightly. Then he was gone.

The room was silent.

Katie stood in the middle of it and felt the weight of everything pressing down on her. The journey. The distance. The strangeness of this place. The knowledge of what waited two hours from now.

Her mother appeared beside her. Put an arm around her shoulders.

"Breathe," Clara said softly. "Just breathe."

Katie breathed.

It did not help as much as she had hoped.

The two hours passed too quickly.

Katie showered in a bathroom larger than her bedroom at home. Changed into clothes her mother had packed. A simple dress. Dark blue. Nothing fancy. Nothing that tried to be something it was not.

She looked at herself in the mirror. Saw a girl who did not belong here. A girl who was about to meet a king.

A knock at the door.

Her heart stopped. Started again too fast.

"Katie?" Her mother's voice. "It's time."

Katie opened the door. Her parents stood in the hallway. Dressed. Ready. Looking as terrified as she felt.

"Together," Thomas said. His voice was rough.

"Together," Katie agreed.

They walked down the hall. Through corridors she did not remember. Past doors that stayed closed. The castle was quiet around them. Waiting.

They reached a door larger than the others. Dark wood. Iron fittings. Frederick stood beside it.

"Miss Parker," he said. "The representatives of the Echo Mark Registry will explain the process before His Majesty arrives. Please enter when ready."

Katie looked at her parents. At the door. At the life she was about to step into.

She pushed the door open and walked through.

The room beyond was warm and well-lit. A table with chairs. Two women seated on one side. One pale and still. One flushed and human.

Not the king. Not yet.

The human woman smiled gently.

"Please sit, Miss Parker. We have much to explain."

Katie sat.

The waiting continued.

But not for much longer.

15

Terms of the Month

The room was smaller than Katie expected.

After the vastness of the halls, the ancient grandeur of everything she had seen, this space felt almost ordinary. A wooden table. Six chairs. A fireplace with a low flame. Windows that showed only darkness now.

The two women sat across from her. The vampire was older than she looked. Katie could feel it somehow. A weight behind her stillness. Eyes that had seen more than any human face could hold.

The human woman was perhaps fifty. Grey at her temples. Kind eyes behind practical glasses. She wore a simple suit. No jewelry except a wedding ring.

Katie's parents took seats on either side of her. Close. Protective. As if their presence could shield her from whatever came next.

"Miss Parker." The human woman spoke first. Her voice was warm. Measured. "My name is Eleanor Hayes. I represent the Echo Mark Registry as a human liaison. This is Elise Frost. She represents the vampire council."

The vampire inclined her head slightly. She did not smile.

"We are not here on behalf of His Majesty," Eleanor continued. "We are neutral parties. Our role is to ensure you understand your rights, your options, and the process that will govern the next month."

Katie nodded. Her throat was too dry to speak.

"First, I want to be very clear about something." Eleanor leaned forward slightly. "Nothing that happens after this meeting is mandatory. The meeting itself is required by law. Your presence here fulfills that requirement. Everything else is your choice."

"My choice," Katie repeated.

"Yes." Eleanor's voice was firm. "You can leave tonight if you wish. You can stay for a day, a week, or the full month. You can meet His Majesty once and never speak to him again. The decision is entirely yours."

Katie felt something loosen in her chest. A tension she had not known she was carrying.

"What happens if I leave?"

"You go home. You resume your life. The match remains on record, but no further action is taken." Eleanor paused. "His Majesty has agreed to these terms. He will not pursue you. He will not contact you. If you choose to leave, that choice is final and respected."

Clara's hand found Katie's under the table. Squeezed.

"And if I stay?"

"Then we begin the courtship period." Eleanor opened a folder in front of her. "One month. During that time, you and His Majesty will have the opportunity to know each other. Conversations. Meals. Time together in supervised and unsupervised settings."

"Unsupervised?" Thomas's voice was sharp.

Elise spoke for the first time. Her voice was cool. Precise. "The courtship period is designed to allow genuine connection. Constant supervision would undermine that purpose. However." She paused. "Miss Parker will have access to staff at all times. She may request accompaniment whenever she wishes. Her private quarters are her own. No one, including His Majesty, may enter without her explicit invitation."

"He won't come to my room?"

"Not unless you ask him to." Elise's expression did not change. "The courtship rules are strict. Physical contact requires verbal consent. Escalation requires mutual agreement. The bond cannot be formed accidentally or through coercion."

Katie absorbed this. The rules were clear. Clearer than she had expected.

"What about my parents?"

"They may stay for the full month," Eleanor said. "Quarters have been prepared for them in this wing. They will have access to you at all times. They may attend meals, join conversations, observe interactions." She smiled slightly. "His Majesty understands that this is unusual. That you have family who love you and want to protect you. He has no desire to separate you from them."

Thomas made a sound. Not quite relief. Not quite acceptance.

"There is additional support available," Eleanor continued. "Medical staff, should you need them. A psychologist on call, should you wish to speak with someone neutral. Access to communications, should you want to contact anyone outside the castle."

"I can call home?"

"Whenever you wish. The castle has full modern amenities despite its age." Eleanor's smile widened slightly. "Hot water, internet, phone service. His Majesty is ancient, but he is not opposed to progress."

Katie almost laughed. Almost.

"Now." Eleanor pulled several documents from her folder. "The courtship agreement. I want to explain each section before you sign anything."

The next hour was paperwork.

Katie had expected something ancient. Parchment and wax seals. Instead, she found modern legal documents. Clear language. Straightforward terms.

The agreement established the timeline. One month from today. At the end, Katie would formally declare her intentions. If she wished to proceed with the bond, a second agreement would be drafted. If she wished to leave, no further obligations existed.

"What is the bond exactly?" Katie asked. "I've read about it, but the descriptions are always vague."

Elise and Eleanor exchanged a glance.

"The mate bond is biological," Elise said. "When a matched pair chooses to formalize their connection, there is a ceremony. An exchange. The bond changes both parties."

"Changes how?"

"The human becomes linked to the vampire. Emotionally. Physically. You would feel his presence. Sense his moods. Know when he is near." Elise paused. "The vampire experiences the same. And there are other changes. Longevity. Health. A resistance to illness and injury that humans do not normally possess."

Katie stared at her. "I would live longer?"

"Bonded humans typically live two to three times longer than average. Some longer still." Elise's voice was matter-of-fact. "The connection sustains. It does not make you immortal. It does not make you vampire. But it extends what you have."

Katie did not know what to say to that.

"The bond cannot be undone," Elise continued. "Once formed, it is permanent. That is why the courtship period exists. That is why consent must be absolute. You must be certain before you agree."

"And he must be certain too," Eleanor added. "The bond works both ways. His Majesty is not simply claiming you. He is binding himself to you as well. Your happiness becomes his concern. Your wellbeing becomes his responsibility."

"What if we don't get along?" Katie asked. "What if we spend a month together and discover we hate each other?"

"Then you do not bond." Elise's voice was calm. "The mark indicates compatibility. It does not guarantee affection. Some matched pairs have chosen to part. It is rare, but it happens."

"And he would accept that?"

"He has agreed to these terms." Elise met Katie's eyes. "I have known William Stone for two centuries. He is not a man who makes promises lightly. If he says he will respect your choice, he will respect your choice."

Katie wanted to believe that. She was not sure she could.

The documents were simpler than she expected. A few pages. Clear sections. Nothing hidden in fine print.

She read each one carefully. Asked questions when she did not understand. Listened to the explanations.

Her parents read over her shoulder. Thomas pointed out clauses. Clara asked about specifics. The representatives answered everything.

Finally, Katie reached the signature line.

"You do not have to sign tonight," Eleanor said. "You can take time. Think about it. We can meet again tomorrow."

Katie looked at the document. At the words that would bind her to nothing except a month of possibility.

She picked up the pen.

"Katie." Thomas's voice was strained. "Are you sure?"

"I'm sure I want to find out." Katie met his eyes. "That's all this is, Dad. Finding out. I can still leave."

She signed her name.

The ink dried slowly.

"Witnessed," Eleanor said, signing below. Elise added her own signature. "The courtship period has officially begun."

Katie set down the pen. Her hand was shaking slightly. She had not noticed until now.

"What happens next?"

Eleanor gathered the documents. "His Majesty is aware that the formalities have concluded. He has requested permission to introduce himself."

Katie's heart stuttered.

"Now?"

"If you are willing. He understands if you prefer to wait until tomorrow."

Katie thought about the hours of travel. The strangeness of this place. The weight of everything she had learned.

She thought about waiting. About another night of not knowing.

"Now," she said. "I'd rather meet him now."

Eleanor nodded. She and Elise rose. Gathered their materials.

"We will send him in," Eleanor said. "Take your time. There is no agenda tonight. No expectations. Simply an introduction."

They moved toward the door. Paused.

"Miss Parker." Elise's voice was softer now. Almost gentle. "I have watched many courtships. Many meetings. This one is unusual. The attention it will receive. The stakes involved. But at its heart, it is simply two people learning whether they might care for each other. Try to remember that."

Katie nodded. She did not trust her voice.

The representatives left.

The room was quiet.

Katie sat with her parents and waited.

The minutes stretched.

Clara straightened Katie's collar. Smoothed her hair. Nervous movements. Motherly movements.

"Whatever happens," Clara said quietly, "we love you."

"I know, Mom."

"He's just a person." Thomas's voice was rough. "Vampire or not. King or not. He's just a person."

Katie was not sure that was true. But she appreciated the attempt.

A knock at the door.

Soft. Almost hesitant.

Katie's breath caught.

"Come in," she heard herself say.

The door opened.

And William Stone stepped into the room.

16

The Castle at Rest

He was taller than she expected.

That was Katie's first thought. Photographs had not captured the way he filled a doorway. The way the space around him seemed to settle into stillness.

He wore dark clothes. Simple. A jacket that might have been expensive or might have been old. She could not tell. His hair was dark, longer than in the formal portraits. His face was pale. His eyes were darker still.

He did not move toward her.

"Miss Parker." His voice was low. Careful. Like someone speaking to a frightened animal. "Thank you for agreeing to see me tonight."

Katie tried to respond. Her throat would not cooperate.

He waited. Patient. Still as stone.

"I know this is overwhelming," he said. "I have had eighteen years to prepare for this moment. You have had less than a day." He paused. "I am grateful that you are here. That you have chosen to stay."

"I signed the agreement," Katie managed. Her voice sounded strange. Thin.

"You signed an agreement to give this time. One month." His expression did not change, but something softened in his eyes. "That is more than I had any right to expect. More than many would give."

He stepped into the room. Slowly. Leaving the door open behind him.

"Your parents." He turned to Clara and Thomas. Inclined his head slightly. "Mr. and Mrs. Parker. I am William Stone. I understand your concern for your daughter. I share it."

Thomas stood. His jaw was tight. His hands were fists at his sides.

"She's our only child," Thomas said. "If you hurt her. If you do anything to make her unhappy."

"Then I would deserve whatever consequences followed." William's voice was calm. Accepting. "I have no intention of hurting her. But I understand that my intentions mean nothing until I have proven them through action."

Thomas stared at him. Searching for something. A tell. A lie.

He did not find one.

"We're staying," Thomas said. "The whole month."

"I would not have it any other way." William turned back to Katie. "I thought, if you are willing, I might show you the castle. Not all of it tonight. That would take days. But enough that you feel less lost."

Katie looked at her parents. At the door. At the vampire king standing in the middle of a room that suddenly felt too small.

"Okay," she said.

They walked through corridors older than her country.

William led. Katie followed a few steps behind. Her parents trailed further back, close enough to see everything, far enough to give the illusion of privacy.

"This wing was built in the thirteenth century," William said. He gestured to the stone walls. The arched ceilings. "Rebuilt twice after fires. The original foundations remain, but most of what you see is newer. Fifteenth century, perhaps. Sixteenth."

Katie touched the wall as she walked. Cold stone beneath her fingertips.

"How long have you lived here?"

"Since my transformation. A little over two hundred years." William glanced back at her. "The castle belonged to my father before me. To his council before him. It has been a seat of power for longer than I can trace."

"Your father." Katie remembered fragments from school. From books. "The old king."

"Yes." Something flickered across William's face. There and gone. "He died before the Accord. Before any of this was possible."

"I'm sorry."

"It was a long time ago." William paused before a set of heavy doors. "The great hall. We do not use it often now. Too large for most purposes. But it is impressive, if you would like to see."

He pushed the doors open.

Katie's breath caught.

The hall stretched before her, vast and shadowed. Stone pillars rose to a ceiling lost in darkness. Windows lined one wall, black with night. At the far end, a raised platform. Thrones. Two of them, side by side.

"State functions," William said. "Formal audiences. The occasional ceremony." His voice held something that might have been irony. "Vampire politics requires spectacle, the same as human politics."

Katie walked further into the hall. Her footsteps echoed. The space made her feel small. Not threatened. Just small.

"It's beautiful," she said.

"It is old." William stood by the door, watching her. "Age accumulates a kind of weight. Beauty is a side effect."

Katie looked at the thrones. Two. Equal in size. Side by side.

"Why two?"

"My father's idea. After he found his mate." William's voice softened. "He said a king without a queen was only half a ruler. So he built a second throne."

Katie did not know what to say to that. She turned away from the thrones.

"What else can you show me?"

They walked for an hour.

William pointed out rooms and explained their purposes. The library, three floors of books, from the ground to the roof. The music room, with instruments no one played anymore. The kitchens, modernized but still using the original stone ovens.

He told her stories as they walked. Not dates and names. Moments. A visiting diplomat who got lost in the east wing for three days. A musician who wrote a symphony in the garden and refused to leave until it was finished. A storm in 1847 that tore off half the roof.

The castle became less strange as he talked. Still vast. Still ancient. But lived in. Real.

"There are areas you should avoid," William said. They had reached a corridor marked by heavier doors. "The north tower is structurally unsound. We are restoring it, but the work is slow. The lower cellars are used for storage, and some of the floors are unsafe."

"Storage," Katie repeated.

"Nothing sinister." A small smile touched his lips. "Old furniture. Documents. The accumulated debris of centuries. Frederick has been cataloguing it for fifty years and believes he might finish sometime in the next century."

Katie found herself smiling back. She had not expected that.

"And the other restricted areas?"

"My private quarters are closed without invitation. As are the council chambers during sessions." William paused. "Beyond that, you are welcome anywhere. The staff know you. They will help if you become lost."

"Will I become lost?"

"Almost certainly." The smile deepened slightly. "The castle has a tendency to rearrange itself in memory. You will learn the paths that matter. The rest reveals itself over time."

They ended in a smaller dining room.

It was warm. Intimate. A table set for four, though Katie had not seen anyone preparing it. Candles burned in iron holders. A fire crackled in the hearth.

"I thought you might be hungry," William said. "Human food. I have already eaten."

Katie's stomach chose that moment to remind her that she had not eaten since the plane.

"I could eat," she admitted.

They sat.

The food appeared in courses, carried by staff who moved quietly and departed without lingering. Simple dishes. Roasted chicken. Vegetables. Fresh bread. Nothing elaborate. Nothing trying to impress.

Katie ate. Her parents ate. William sat with them, a glass of something dark in front of him that he did not drink.

"Can I ask you something?" Katie said.

"Anything."

"Blood." She felt her face heat. "You said you'd already eaten. But you can eat food too. Regular food."

"Yes." William turned his glass slowly. "Blood is necessary for survival. Without it, we weaken. Eventually, we become incapable of functioning. But food." He paused. "Food is different."

"Different how?"

"Blood sustains the body. Food sustains the memory." He looked at his glass. "I do not need to eat bread. But I remember the taste from my human years. I remember my mother baking it in our kitchen. Eating it warm from the oven." Something distant crossed his face. "Food is connection. To who we were. To the humans we live among. It reminds us that we are not only predators."

Katie had not expected that answer. Had not expected the sadness beneath it.

"Your mother was human."

"Yes. She lived to be only eighty. She ate dinner with my father every night until the end." William set down his glass. "He did not need the food. But he needed the ritual. The time together."

The room was quiet.

"That's why you built the Accord," Katie said slowly. "The registry. The rules. Because of them."

"In part." William met her eyes. "I watched my father wait eight hundred years for her. I watched him love her for fifty-five. I watched him mourn her for the decades after." He paused. "I did not want to wait in silence. I did not want to spend centuries wondering if my match existed, if she was safe, if I would ever have the chance to know her. The old way was not sustainable. It never was."

Katie thought about that.

"You've been waiting since I was born," she said, though she knew the answer.

"Yes."

"That must have been difficult."

"It was necessary." William's voice was quiet. "You deserved a childhood. A normal life. Time to become who you were meant to be without the weight of me pressing down on you. The waiting was not difficult. It was the least I could offer."

Katie did not know how to respond. She looked down at her plate instead.

The meal ended quietly.

William stood as the staff cleared the dishes. He moved to the door, then paused.

"Tomorrow, if you are willing, we could continue. There is much more of the castle to see. And more questions you might want to ask."

"I'd like that," Katie said.

William nodded. Something eased in his posture. Relief, perhaps. Or the beginning of it.

"I rise at sunset. Until then, the castle is yours. The staff will attend you. Your parents may go where they wish." He paused at the threshold. "Sleep well, Miss Parker. I am glad you are here."

He left before she could respond.

The door closed softly behind him.

Katie sat in the warmth of the small dining room and felt something shift in her chest. Not trust, exactly. Not yet.

But something. The first faint stirring of something.

"Well," Clara said quietly. "That was not what I expected."

"No," Katie agreed. "It wasn't."

Thomas was silent for a long moment. Then he exhaled slowly.

"I still don't like it," he said. "But I think you may be right, I don't detect that you are in any danger with him."

Katie looked at the door where William had disappeared.

One month, she thought. One month to figure out what this was. What it could be.

Tomorrow, she would learn more. Ask more. Try to understand the ancient creature who had waited two hundred years for her.

Tonight, she would sleep.

17

Two Time Zones

William stood at the window of his chambers and watched the last light fade from the sky.

She was here.

After eighteen years of waiting. After two centuries of solitude. She was here, in his castle, sleeping in a room three corridors away.

He could feel her.

That was what he had not expected. The pull. The quiet, insistent awareness of her presence, like a compass pointing north. He had read about it, of course. Heard other vampires describe the sensation when they found their match. But reading was not the same as knowing.

She was his mate. There was no doubt now. The mark had told him she existed. His blood told him she was real.

He closed his eyes and let himself remember.

Her face when he walked into the room. The way fear had flickered across her features and then steadied into something else. Curiosity, perhaps. Or determination. She had not frozen. Had not gone silent the way so many humans did in the presence of vampires. He had seen that reaction countless times over the centuries. The primitive part of the brain recognizing predator, shutting down higher functions, leaving nothing but trembling silence.

Katie had trembled. But she had spoken. Asked questions. Listened to his answers with eyes that missed nothing.

She was beautiful. He had known she would be. Not because the bond required beauty, but because he had spent eighteen years imagining her, and imagination always fell short of reality. Brown hair that caught the firelight. Blue eyes that held depths he wanted to explore. A face that showed everything she felt, even when she tried to hide it.

And intelligent. That mattered more than beauty, in the end. She had asked about the thrones. About his mother. About the food and the blood and the difference between them. She had not accepted surface answers. She had pushed deeper.

He had not expected that. Had prepared himself for awkwardness, for silence, for the slow work of drawing someone out of their shell. Instead, he had found a woman who was already reaching toward understanding.

The fear was there. He did not fool himself about that. She was afraid of him. Of this place. Of what might happen over the next month. But her fear was the sensible kind. The fear of the unknown. Not the terror of prey.

William opened his eyes. The sky was dark now. The stars were emerging.

She would be sleeping. Humans kept different hours. Tomorrow, they would need to discuss that. Find a way to bridge the gap between his nights and her days.

For now, he would wait. He had waited eighteen years. He could wait a few more hours.

The pull remained. Constant. Patient.

She was here.

That was all that mattered.

Katie woke to sunlight.

For a moment, she did not know where she was. The ceiling was too high. The bed was too soft. The air smelled of old stone and wood smoke instead of the familiar mustiness of home.

Then she remembered.

She lay still and let the memories settle. The journey. The meeting. The vampire king who had walked into her life and somehow made it larger.

A knock at the door.

"Katie?" Her mother's voice. "Breakfast is ready."

Katie pulled herself out of bed. Found clothes. Made herself presentable. The room was cold, but a fire had been lit in the hearth while she slept. She had not heard anyone enter.

The sitting room of their suite was warm and bright. A table had been set near the windows. Her parents were already there, cups of coffee in their hands.

"Sleep well?" Thomas asked.

"Better than I expected." Katie sat down. Reached for the coffee pot. "You?"

"The bed is too comfortable." Thomas's voice carried a hint of his old humor.

Clara smiled. "Nothing went wrong. I think that might be the strangest part."

Katie looked around the room. A woman was clearing dishes from a sideboard. Human. Middle-aged. Moving with the quiet efficiency of someone who had done this work for years.

Katie thought about the night before. The staff who had served dinner. The ones who had guided them through the halls.

All human.

"The servants," she said slowly. "Are they all human?"

Clara nodded. "I noticed that too. I asked one of them this morning. Apparently the day staff is entirely human. The vampires work at night."

"That makes sense." Katie poured her coffee. "Sunlight."

"It's thoughtful," Clara said. "Having humans around during the day. It makes this place feel less..."

"Alien," Thomas finished.

"I was going to say intimidating. But yes."

Katie ate breakfast and thought about that. The king had built a world where humans could move through his castle without fear. Where the ancient and the modern existed side by side. Where a girl from Pennsylvania could wake up in a Scottish fortress and find coffee waiting.

It was strange. But it was also, in its own way, considerate.

After breakfast, Katie explored.

Her parents came with her at first. They walked through the halls William had shown her the night before, seeing them now in daylight. The stone walls glowed golden where the sun touched them. The tapestries revealed colors that had been hidden in candlelight. The castle felt different. Older, somehow. More real.

After an hour, her parents retreated to their room. Thomas wanted to rest. Clara wanted to call home and check on things. Katie understood. This was exhausting for all of them.

She kept walking.

The castle was a maze. Corridors branched into corridors. Stairs led up and down without apparent logic. Doors opened onto rooms she had not expected.

She found a music room with a grand piano covered in dust. A gallery of weapons that looked too old to be real. A conservatory with plants she could not name, green and thriving despite the grey sky outside.

And then she found the portraits.

They hung in a long gallery on the second floor. Paintings stretching back centuries. Men and women with pale skin and dark eyes. The vampire court, she realized. Kings and queens and advisors, captured in oil and canvas.

She walked slowly along the gallery. Studied each face. Tried to find William among them.

She found him near the end. Younger in the painting, though she could not have said how she knew. The same dark hair. The same careful eyes. But something less guarded in his expression. Something that had not yet learned to hide itself.

Beside his portrait hung another. A woman. Human, Katie thought. Something in the warmth of her skin, the softness of her features. She had dark hair and kind eyes and a smile that seemed to hold secrets.

A small plaque beneath the frame read: Margaret Stone, Queen Consort.

His mother.

Katie stared at the portrait. The woman had lived to be eighty, William had said. A full human lifespan. But she had been mated to a vampire king. Bonded. Connected.

If the bond extended life, why had she died so young?

And his father. The old king. William had said he died before the Accord. But vampires were indestructible. That was the whole point. Human weapons could not harm them. Human methods could not kill them.

So how had the old king died?

Katie filed the questions away. They felt too heavy for casual conversation. Too personal for someone she had known less than a day.

She would ask eventually. When the time was right.

She kept walking.

The library found her by accident.

She had been looking for a way back to the family wing. Taken a wrong turn, then another. And suddenly she was standing in a doorway, looking at more books than she had ever seen in one place.

Three floors. William had mentioned that. But she had not understood what it meant until now.

The room stretched upward into shadows. Galleries ringed each level, connected by spiral staircases that looked too delicate to hold weight. Books lined every wall. Old books. New books. Books in languages she could not read.

Katie stepped inside. The air smelled of paper and dust and something faintly sweet. Lavender, maybe. Or old leather.

She wandered through the stacks. Ran her fingers along spines. Pulled out volumes at random and flipped through pages yellow with age.

History. Philosophy. Poetry. Fiction. The collection was vast and varied. Someone had spent centuries gathering these books. Caring for them. Arranging them on shelves where they would be found by wandering visitors.

Katie found a section of novels near a window. English. Mostly nineteenth century. She recognized some of the authors. Others were unfamiliar.

She pulled out a book at random. Settled into a chair by the window. Started to read.

The light shifted as the afternoon passed. Grey to gold to grey again. The castle was quiet around her. The book was good. Absorbing. A story about a woman in a house full of secrets.

Katie's eyes grew heavy.

She told herself she would rest them for just a moment.

She fell asleep.

William woke at sunset.

The awareness of her was immediate. Constant. A presence in the back of his mind that had not been there before yesterday.

He rose. Dressed. Prepared himself for the evening ahead.

The staff had reported her movements through the day. Breakfast with her parents. Exploration of the castle. Time in the portrait gallery, where she had lingered before his mother's image.

And now the library. She had been there for hours.

William followed the pull.

The castle was quiet at this hour. The transition between day and night, when human staff retreated and vampire staff emerged. He moved through the halls without sound. Habit, more than intention.

The library doors stood open.

He found her in a chair by the window. The book had fallen to her lap. Her head was tilted against the chair's high back. Her breathing was slow and even.

Asleep.

William stood in the doorway and watched her. The way the fading light touched her hair. The slight furrow between her brows, as if her dreams were puzzling her. The vulnerability of her posture, unguarded in a way she had not been the night before.

She was beautiful.

He had thought so last night. He thought so now. But it was a different kind of beauty in sleep. Softer. More human.

He could have let her rest. Could have retreated and returned later. But she would wake disoriented, not knowing how much time had passed or where she was.

He crossed to her chair. Knelt beside it. Reached out and touched her shoulder.

Gently. Carefully. The lightest pressure he could manage.

"Miss Parker."

She stirred. Her eyes opened slowly. Confusion first, then recognition, then embarrassment.

"I fell asleep." Her voice was rough with sleep. She sat up quickly, the book tumbling to the floor. "I'm sorry. I didn't mean to."

"There is nothing to apologize for." William retrieved the book. Glanced at the cover. "You have good taste. This is one of my favorites."

"Really?" Katie rubbed her eyes. "I didn't finish it."

"You have a month." He set the book on the table beside her chair. "Dinner is being prepared, if you are hungry."

Katie nodded. She was still blinking away sleep, her hair slightly mussed, her dress creased from the chair. She looked young. Uncertain. Very far from home.

William stepped back. Gave her space.

"Take your time," he said. "I will wait in the hall."

She joined him a few minutes later. Her hair was smoothed. Her composure restored. But he could still see traces of sleep in the softness of her expression.

They walked to the small dining room together. Her parents were already there, seated at the table, looking well-rested if still wary.

Dinner was quiet.

Katie ate. Her parents ate. William sat with them, as he had the night before. He answered questions when they were asked. Offered information when it seemed welcome.

After the meal, he rose.

"I thought we might continue the tour," he said. "If you are willing. There are parts of the castle I did not have time to show you last night."

Katie stood. "I'd like that."

They walked through the east wing first.

Katie asked questions as they went. Not about his family. Not about the personal things. About the castle itself. The history of its construction. The purpose of rooms they passed.

She had been paying attention during the day. He could tell. She pointed out architectural details she had noticed. Asked about paintings she had seen. Wondered about the purpose of a courtyard she had glimpsed from a window.

William answered everything. He found himself talking more than he usually did. Telling stories he had not thought about in decades. Making her laugh, once, with an account of a visiting dignitary who had challenged Frederick to a duel and spent the next week apologizing.

They reached the west tower as the night deepened.

Katie paused at a window. Looked out at the stars.

And yawned.

She covered her mouth quickly. "I'm sorry. That's so rude."

"It is not rude. It is biology." William moved to stand beside her. Not too close. "You are exhausted."

"I slept on the plane. And in the library."

"Neither of which is the same as proper rest." He paused. "This is one of the challenges we face, you and I. I sleep during the day. You sleep at night. Our hours barely overlap."

Katie nodded slowly. "I noticed that. Yesterday you said you rise at sunset."

"And sleep at dawn. Most vampires keep the same schedule." He looked out at the darkness. "It makes courtship difficult. We have only the edges of our days in common."

"What do other Echo Mark pairs do?"

"They adapt. One or both adjusts their schedule. It is not comfortable at first, but humans are remarkably flexible." He turned to face her. "I would not ask you to abandon daylight entirely. But if you were willing to shift your sleep. Rise later. Stay awake longer. We would have more time together."

Katie considered this. He watched the thoughts move behind her eyes.

"That makes sense," she said finally. "I'm here to get to know you. It's hard to do that if we're awake at different times."

"Is that a yes?"

"That's a yes." She smiled. Small but genuine. "I can't promise I won't yawn."

"I can live with yawning." Something eased in his chest. Relief, perhaps. Or gratitude. "Tomorrow, sleep as late as you wish. I will have breakfast waiting when you wake."

"Breakfast at sunset."

"Breakfast whenever you need it." He gestured toward the corridor. "For tonight, let me escort you back to your quarters. You need rest more than you need another hour of hallways."

They walked back through the castle. The silence between them was comfortable now. Less careful than it had been the night before.

At the door to the family wing, William stopped.

"Thank you," he said. "For today. For this conversation. For agreeing to adjust your schedule."

"Thank you for being patient with me." Katie hesitated. "This is all very strange. But you're making it less strange. If that makes sense."

"It makes perfect sense." He inclined his head slightly. "Sleep well, Miss Parker."

"Katie," she said. "You can call me Katie."

Something shifted in his expression. Softened.

"Sleep well, Katie."

She smiled. Disappeared through the door.

William stood in the empty corridor and listened to her footsteps fade.

Katie.

It was a small thing. A gesture of trust. But it meant more to him than she could know.

He turned and walked back toward his own chambers. The pull went with him. Constant. Patient.

She was here. She was staying so far. She had smiled at him and asked to be called Katie, not Kathryn, but Katie.

Tomorrow, they would have more time.

18

The First Week

The new schedule took three days to feel normal.

Katie slept until early afternoon. Woke to grey Scottish light filtering through her curtains. Had breakfast while her parents had lunch. Spent the late afternoon reading or exploring or sitting with her mother in the conservatory, watching rain streak the glass.

And then, at sunset, William appeared.

They fell into a rhythm. Dinner first, with her parents. Conversation kept light, topics kept safe. Then the evening stretched before them, hours of time that belonged to no one else.

On the fourth night, he taught her to play chess.

"You've never played?" William set the board between them. They were in a small sitting room off the library, fire crackling in the hearth, rain tapping at the windows.

"We had checkers at home. Does that count?"

"It does not count." But he was smiling. "Chess is older than most civilizations. It teaches patience, strategy, sacrifice. The willingness to lose a piece now for advantage later."

"So it's like life."

"It is very much like life." He began arranging the pieces. "Except in chess, you can see all the moves. In life, half the board is hidden."

Katie watched his hands. Long fingers. Precise movements. He handled each piece as if it mattered.

"White moves first," he said. "That's you."

"Why me?"

"Because I have been playing for two hundred years and you have been playing for four minutes. You need every advantage."

Katie laughed. It surprised her, the ease of it. "That's not very encouraging."

"I am being realistic. You will lose. Probably badly. But you will learn something in the losing." He gestured to the board. "Your move."

She lost. Badly. In eleven moves.

"That was embarrassing," she said.

"That was a beginning." William reset the pieces. "Again."

She lost the second game in fifteen moves. The third in twenty-two. By the fourth, she was starting to see patterns. Starting to understand why he moved certain pieces certain ways.

"You're letting me last longer," she accused.

"I am letting you learn." He captured her queen with a knight she had forgotten about. "There is a difference."

"Is there?"

"If I crushed you immediately every time, you would stop playing. If I let you believe you are improving, you will continue." He smiled. "Both outcomes serve my purposes."

"Your purposes being?"

"Continued access to your company." He said it lightly. But something flickered in his eyes. Something that was not entirely a joke.

Katie looked at the board. Moved a pawn. Tried not to think too hard about what he had said.

The fifth night, they talked about his parents.

It started with a question. Katie had been thinking about it for days, ever since the portrait gallery. The words had been building behind her teeth, waiting for the right moment.

They were in the library. William had found a book he wanted to show her, something about the history of the Highlands. They sat in chairs by the fire, the book forgotten on the table between them.

"Can I ask you something personal?" Katie said.

"You can ask me anything."

"Your parents." She hesitated. "How did they meet?"

William was quiet for a moment. The fire popped. Shadows moved across his face.

"The old way," he said finally. "Before the registry. Before any system at all." He leaned back in his chair. "My father was nearly eight hundred years old when she was born. He had spent centuries believing he would never find his match. That he would exist forever, alone, waiting for something that might not exist."

"Eight hundred years." Katie could not imagine it. Could barely grasp the shape of that much time.

"He had given up hope. That was what he told me later. He had made peace with solitude. Built a life that did not require a mate. And then one day, walking through a village in Wales, he felt it."

"The pull."

"Yes. Immediate. Overwhelming. He said it was like a hook in his chest, dragging him toward a cottage at the edge of town." William's voice softened. "She was inside. Margaret. Nineteen years old. Dark hair, dark eyes. She had a mark on her shoulder that matched the one he had carried for eight centuries."

Katie listened. The fire crackled. The rain continued its quiet percussion against the windows.

"He did not approach her that day. He watched from a distance. Learned who she was. Discovered that she was kind and clever and stubborn. That she argued with her father about politics. That she read books when she should have been working. That she laughed easily and often."

"How long did he watch?"

"A year." William smiled slightly. "He was terrified. Eight hundred years of waiting, and he was afraid she would reject him. That she would see a monster instead of a mate."

"But she didn't."

"She did not. When he finally introduced himself, she looked at him for a long moment. Then she said, 'You're the one who's been lurking near the mill. I was wondering when you'd find your courage.'"

Katie laughed. She could not help it. "She sounds formidable."

"She was. She was also kind, and patient, and completely unimpressed by his age or his power." William's voice grew distant. "They had fifty-five years together. He said it was worth eight hundred years of waiting. He meant it."

The fire settled. A log collapsed into embers.

Katie gathered her courage. "How did he die?"

William did not answer immediately. His expression did not change, but something behind his eyes went still.

"Another vampire," he said. "My father was walking the grounds one evening. Alone. He often did that, after my mother passed. Said it helped him think." He paused. "A vampire came out of the darkness. Attacked without warning. By the time the guards reached them, it was over."

Katie felt cold. "I thought vampires were indestructible."

"To humans. Not to each other." William's voice was flat. "Only a vampire can kill a vampire. It requires physical destruction. Tearing the body apart. Separating head and heart." He looked into the fire. "This vampire was old. Older than my father. He knew exactly what he was doing."

"Why?"

"He blamed my father for the failures of the old Echo system. The one we used before the registry." William's jaw tightened. "He was fifteen hundred years old. He had just received word that his mate had been identified. A woman in Portugal. He travelled there immediately."

Katie waited.

"She had been dead for twenty years." William's voice was quiet. "The system had failed. The information came too late. He had waited fifteen centuries, and when he finally learned where his mate was, she was already gone."

Katie's chest ached. She thought about fifteen hundred years. About hope deferred so long it became its own kind of torture. About arriving at the end of all that waiting to find nothing but a grave.

"He felt robbed," William said. "And he was. The old system was broken. We knew it was broken. We did not fix it fast enough." He paused. "What he did was wrong. Murder is wrong. But I understood his rage. I felt for him, even as I tracked him down."

"You found him."

"I found him. I administered the punishment myself." William's voice held no satisfaction. No triumph. Just weariness. "It did not bring my father back. It did not fix the system. It was simply the law, applied as it had to be applied."

Katie did not know what to say. She sat with the silence, letting it fill the space between them.

"I'm sorry," she said finally. "For all of it."

William nodded. He did not look at her. "It was a long time ago. But thank you."

"And your mother?" Katie asked softly. "You said she lived to eighty. But I thought the bond extended life."

"It does. When the bond is complete." William turned to face her. "My parents did not complete the bond. They did not know how."

"What do you mean?"

"At the time, we understood the marks. The pull. We thought that was all there was. That recognition was enough." He shook his head. "It was not until fifty years after my mother died that we discovered the rest. The exchange."

"Exchange?"

"Blood." William said it simply. "To complete the bond, there must be an exchange of blood. The human drinks from the vampire. The vampire drinks from the human. It is a small amount. Less than a blood donation. But without it, the bond remains incomplete. The human ages normally. Lives a normal span."

Katie felt something cold settle in her stomach. "Blood."

"Yes." William was watching her carefully. "I can see that unsettles you."

"A little." She tried to keep her voice steady. "The idea of being bitten. Of drinking blood."

"I understand. It sounds frightening. Violent, perhaps." He leaned forward slightly. "But I promise you, it is neither. A bite from a mate does not hurt. The bond changes the experience entirely. And vampire blood is not what you might imagine. Other humans have described it as sweet. Like a sugary drink."

Katie nodded slowly. She was not reassured. Not entirely.

"Katie." William's voice was gentle. "We are a very long way from that. We have barely begun to know each other. The ceremony, the bond, all of it. That is months away, if it happens at all." He paused. "I did not tell you this to frighten you. I told you because you asked, and I will not lie to you. But please. Do not let it weigh on you. Let us focus on now. On learning who we are to each other."

She met his eyes. Found nothing there but patience. Honesty. The willingness to wait.

She was starting to understand why his people followed him.

The sixth night, she told him about home.

They were playing chess again. She was getting better. Still losing, but lasting longer. Learning to see three moves ahead instead of one.

"Your family," William said. He moved his bishop. "You have not spoken much about them. Beyond the obvious."

Katie considered the board. Moved a knight. "What do you want to know?"

"Whatever you wish to tell me."

She was quiet for a moment. Thinking about home. About the house that always needed repairs. About the bills on the kitchen counter. About the way her parents smiled even when they were tired.

"We don't have much," she said finally. "Money, I mean. We've never had much."

William did not respond. Just listened.

"My dad lost his job when I was thirteen. Found another one, but it paid less. My mom works too, but there's never quite enough." Katie captured one of his pawns. A small victory. "I used to lie awake at night and listen to them talk about bills. About what they could afford and what they couldn't. They tried to hide it from me, but I heard."

"That must have been difficult."

"It was. It is." She looked up at him. "That's one of the things I keep thinking about. Being here, in this castle. With servants and private jets and food that appears whenever I want it. And my parents are home in a house with a leaky roof, worrying about the heating bill."

"They are here. With you."

"For now. But eventually they'll go back. And I'll be..." She trailed off.

William was quiet for a long moment. He studied the board, but she could tell he was not thinking about chess.

"Katie," he said finally. "Regardless of what happens between us. Regardless of what you decide at the end of this month. Your parents will never worry about money again."

She stared at him. "What?"

"I mean it. Whatever they need. The roof. The bills. Medical care. Education, if you want to continue your studies." He met her eyes. "What is mine is yours. That is not contingent on your choice. It is simply true."

"You can't do that."

"I can. I will." His voice was calm. Certain. "You are my match. Your family is my family. Whether you become my mate or not, that connection exists. I will honor it."

Katie felt tears prick her eyes. She blinked them back.

"Why?" she asked. "Why would you do that when I might say no? When I might walk away?"

"Because it is the right thing to do." William moved a rook. "Because your parents raised you, loved you, made you who you are. Because they are here, in a strange place, trusting me with their daughter. Because they deserve security regardless of how their daughter's story ends."

Katie did not know what to say. The chess game sat forgotten between them.

"Thank you," she managed. Her voice was thick.

"You do not need to thank me. You do not need to feel obligated." He smiled slightly. "Consider it a bribe, if it makes you feel better."

She laughed despite herself. "A bribe?"

"I am trying to impress you. Is it working?"

"A little."

"Then it was worth every penny." He gestured to the board. "Your move. And I should warn you, I am about to win."

She looked at the board. Saw the trap she had walked into three moves ago.

"That's cheating."

"That is chess. There is a difference."

"You keep saying that."

"Because it keeps being true." He captured her king with a flourish. "Checkmate."

Katie groaned. But she was smiling.

"Again?" William asked.

"Again," she agreed.

They played three more games. She lost all of them. But each loss lasted longer than the one before.

Progress, she thought. Slow and steady.

Like everything else between them.

On the seventh night, they did not play chess.

They sat by the fire in the small sitting room and simply talked. About books they had read. About places they wanted to see. About the differences between American and Scottish weather, which led to a debate about the superiority of various types of rain.

"Rain is rain," Katie argued.

"Rain is absolutely not rain. Scottish rain has character. American rain is simply wet."

"That's the most pretentious thing you've ever said."

"I have said far more pretentious things. You simply have not been around long enough to hear them."

Katie threw a cushion at him.

He caught it without looking. Set it neatly aside.

"Your reflexes are annoying," she said.

"My reflexes are excellent. There is a difference."

"You have got to stop saying that."

"When it stops being true, I will stop saying it." He smiled. "Until then, you are simply going to have to accept my superior wisdom."

"Superior wisdom. From a man who spent ten minutes yesterday explaining why Highland cattle are philosophers."

"They are philosophers. Their contemplation of grass is deeply meaningful."

"Their contemplation of grass is eating."

"Eating can be meaningful. You have clearly never had a truly excellent sandwich."

Katie laughed until her sides hurt.

This, she thought. This was what she had not expected. The ease of it. The comfort. He was ancient and powerful and strange, and somehow he was also the easiest person she had ever talked to.

"Thank you," she said when the laughter faded.

"For what?"

"For this week. For being patient. For making this less terrifying than I expected."

William's expression softened. "You have nothing to thank me for. This week has been a gift. Your company. Your questions. Your willingness to throw cushions at a king."

"Is that a criticism?"

"It is an observation. Kings are rarely assaulted with soft furnishings. It is refreshing."

"I could throw something harder."

"Please do not. I have grown fond of my current skull shape."

Katie smiled. The fire crackled. The rain continued outside, steady and endless.

One week down, she thought. Three to go.

She did not know what would happen. Did not know who she would be at the end of this.

But sitting here, in the warmth and the quiet, she thought she might be starting to find out.

19

Pride and Silence

Katie found her parents in the conservatory. It was early afternoon, grey light filtering through the glass walls, rain tracing patterns down the panes. Her mother sat in a wicker chair, a book open in her lap. Her father stood at the window, staring out at the gardens.

He looked tired. Katie noticed it immediately. The set of his shoulders. The way he held himself, like something was weighing on him.

"Dad?"

Thomas turned. His expression shifted, tried to smooth itself into something neutral. He did not quite succeed.

"Katie. You're up early."

"Couldn't sleep." She crossed to stand beside him. "What's wrong?"

"Nothing's wrong."

"Dad."

He sighed. Looked back out at the rain.

"I called the shop this morning," he said. "Talked to my manager. He said they're cutting hours. Maybe laying people off." He paused. "I've been gone two weeks. That's not a good look."

Katie felt her stomach tighten. "They can't fire you for this. The Echo Mark summons is legally protected."

"Protected doesn't mean safe. They can find other reasons if they want to." Thomas shook his head. "I've been thinking. Maybe I should go home. Make sure I still have something to go back to."

"Thomas." Clara's voice was quiet. "We talked about this."

"I know what we talked about. But talking doesn't pay the mortgage."

Katie looked between her parents. The worry in her mother's face. The stubborn set of her father's jaw.

"Actually," she said slowly, "that's something I need to tell you."

She told them.

About William's promise. About the support he had offered. About the words that had lodged in her chest and stayed there: What is mine is yours. That is not contingent on your choice.

Her mother listened in silence. Her father's expression went through several transformations. Surprise. Disbelief. And then something harder.

"No," Thomas said.

"Dad."

"I said no." His voice was tight. "We don't need his charity. We've managed fine on our own."

"You were just talking about losing your job."

"That's different. That's life. We handle it. We don't take handouts from some vampire king who thinks he can buy us."

"He's not trying to buy us." Katie felt frustration rising. "He's trying to help."

"It's the same thing."

"It's really not."

"Thomas." Clara set down her book. Stood. "At least think about it."

"I have thought about it. I've been thinking about nothing else since we got here." Thomas turned away from the window. "This castle. The servants. The private jets. All of it. We don't belong here, Clara. We're not these people."

"No one is asking us to be."

"Aren't they?" Thomas looked at Katie. His eyes were hard, but something vulnerable flickered beneath. "This is your decision, Katie. Whatever you choose, your mother and I will support you. But I won't let some stranger pay our bills because he wants something from my daughter."

Katie opened her mouth to argue. Closed it again.

She did not know what to say that would reach him.

Thomas walked out of the conservatory. The door closed behind him with a sound that was not quite a slam.

Clara sighed. "Give him time. He's scared."

"Of what?"

"Of losing you. Of this world that's bigger than anything he knows how to handle." Clara crossed to Katie. Took her hands. "He's a proud man. It's one of the things I love about him. But sometimes pride makes it hard to see clearly."

"What do I do?"

"Nothing. Let him work through it." Clara squeezed her hands. "The king's offer is generous. More than generous. But your father needs to come to terms with it in his own way."

Katie nodded. She did not feel reassured.

Thomas found William the next evening.

Katie heard about it later, pieced together from fragments. Her father had asked Frederick where the king could be found. Had walked through the castle with the determination of a man going into battle.

He found William in the study. Reading. Alone.

"Mr. Parker." William set aside his book. "Please, come in."

Thomas did not sit. He stood in the center of the room, hands at his sides, chin raised.

"I need to talk to you," he said.

"Of course."

"About your offer. The money. The support." Thomas's voice was controlled. Careful. "I appreciate the gesture. But I can't accept it."

William studied him for a moment. His expression revealed nothing.

"May I ask why?"

"Because we don't take charity. Clara and I have worked for everything we have. It's not much, but it's ours. We earned it." Thomas squared his shoulders. "I won't let my daughter feel like she owes you something. Like we owe you something."

William was quiet. The fire crackled in the hearth.

"You are a fool," he said.

Thomas stiffened. "Excuse me?"

"I said you are a fool." William's voice was calm. Almost gentle. "You are allowing pride to make decisions that will hurt your family."

"My pride has kept my family together for twenty years."

"Your pride has also kept them struggling." William stood. Moved to face Thomas directly. "I have watched Katie this past week. Listened to her. She worries about you. About your wife. About the house with the leaky roof and the bills that never quite get paid. That worry lives in her constantly. It shapes her choices. It limits her dreams."

Thomas said nothing. His jaw was tight.

"I am offering to remove that worry. Not as charity. Not as payment. Simply because she is my match, and your wellbeing is part of hers." William paused. "Does your daughter not deserve to have anything she desires? To dream without constraint? To build a life without the weight of financial fear pressing down on her?"

"Of course she deserves that."

"Then why would you take it away from her?" William's voice hardened slightly. "Because of pride? Because accepting help feels like weakness?" He shook his head. "There is nothing weak about providing for your family. There is nothing shameful about accepting what is freely given."

Thomas stared at him. Something shifted behind his eyes.

"If Katie chooses to leave at the end of this month," William continued, "she will leave with security. Her family will be protected. Her future will be stable. That is not negotiable. It is not dependent on her feelings for me. It simply is."

"Why?" Thomas's voice was rough. "Why would you do that when she might walk away?"

"Because I have waited two hundred years for her. Because her happiness matters more to me than my own. Because you raised her, loved her, made her the woman she is." William met his eyes. "You are her family. That makes you my family. And I take care of my family."

The room was silent.

Thomas looked at the fire. At the shelves of ancient books. At the vampire king standing before him with patience written into every line of his body.

"I don't know how to do this," Thomas said finally. His voice had lost its edge. "How to be here. How to accept all of this. It's not the world I know."

"No. It is not." William's voice softened. "But you are learning. You are trying. That is all anyone can ask."

Thomas was quiet for a long moment.

"Thank you," he said. The words sounded like they cost him something.

"You do not need to thank me. You need to take care of your daughter. Let me worry about the rest."

Thomas nodded slowly. He looked at William with something that was not quite trust but might become it.

"She's lucky," he said. "To have someone who cares about her this much."

"I am the lucky one," William replied. "She is remarkable. But I suspect you already know that."

For the first time since arriving at the castle, Thomas almost smiled.

"Yeah," he said. "I know."

The council dinner happened three nights later.

Katie had not expected to attend. She knew William had advisors, councils, responsibilities that existed apart from their courtship. She had assumed those worlds would remain separate.

But he had asked her to come. Said he wanted her to see this part of his life. To understand what it meant to rule.

She should have said no.

The dining hall was formal. Larger than the room where they usually ate. A long table filled with vampires she did not recognize. Frederick sat near the head, his ancient face unreadable. Vivian was there too, sharp-eyed and watchful. Others she had glimpsed in the halls but never met.

Katie sat at William's right hand. Her parents had been invited too, but Thomas had declined. Said this was her world to learn, not his.

She wished he had come.

The conversation moved quickly. Politics. Territories. Disputes she did not understand. William listened more than he spoke, interjecting occasionally to clarify or redirect.

Katie tried to follow. Tried to understand the currents beneath the words. But the references were unfamiliar. The history was missing. She felt like someone reading a book from the middle, pages torn out before and after.

She stayed quiet. Watched. Listened.

And then William turned to her.

"Katie." His voice cut through the discussion. "What do you think?"

The table went silent.

Katie felt the weight of their attention. A dozen pairs of eyes, old and knowing, fixed on her face.

"I... I'm not sure I understand the issue well enough to comment," she said carefully.

"The issue is territorial expansion in the Nordic regions. Whether we should support the current boundaries or advocate for revision." William's tone was encouraging. "You have been listening. What is your instinct?"

Katie thought about what she had heard. The arguments on both sides. The tensions she had sensed beneath the polite words.

"It seems like the current boundaries cause more problems than they solve," she said slowly. "But changing them would require trust that doesn't exist yet. Maybe the question isn't which boundaries are right. Maybe it's how to build enough trust to make any boundary work."

William nodded. Something like approval flickered in his expression.

And then a voice from down the table. Male. Ancient. Dripping with condescension.

"Your Majesty, with respect. Why would you seek a little girl's opinion on a matter of state?"

Katie felt the words like a slap.

She looked at the speaker. A vampire with silver hair and cold eyes. He was not looking at her. He was looking at William. As if she were not even worth addressing directly.

William's expression did not change. But something stilled behind his eyes.

"You make a fair point, Samuel," he said. "My apologies. Let us continue."

The conversation moved on. Katie heard none of it.

A little girl. He had called her a little girl, and William had apologized. Had let it pass. Had not defended her.

She sat through the rest of the dinner in silence. Ate nothing. Spoke to no one. Counted the minutes until she could leave.

When the meal finally ended, she did not wait for William. She stood, murmured something about being tired, and walked out of the room.

She made it to her quarters before the tears came.

What Katie did not see happened in the corridor outside the dining hall.

William waited until the other council members had dispersed. Then he caught Samuel's arm.

"A word."

Samuel turned. He was old. Eight hundred years, perhaps. He had served on the council for three centuries. He was accustomed to deference.

He did not find it in William's face.

"Your Majesty?"

"That woman is to be Queen Consort." William's voice was low. Controlled. Ice beneath the surface. "She is not a little girl. She is not a curiosity. She is my mate, and she deserves the respect that position commands."

Samuel's expression flickered. "I meant no disrespect. I simply—"

"You meant to remind me of her age. Her inexperience. Her humanity." William stepped closer. "I am aware of all those things. They do not diminish her. They do not make her opinions worthless."

"She knows nothing of our politics."

"She knows nothing because she has not been taught. How is she to learn if we do not include her? How is she to grow into her role if she is dismissed before she can begin?" William's grip tightened on Samuel's arm. "She will be queen, Samuel. Long after you have faded from this council, she will be at my side. I suggest you remember that."

Samuel swallowed. Nodded.

"It will not happen again, Your Majesty."

"No. It will not."

William released him. Turned and walked toward the family wing.

But when he reached Katie's door, he found it closed. Locked. Silence beyond.

He did not knock. She needed space. She needed time.

He would explain tomorrow. Make her understand that he had not agreed with Samuel. That his silence in the moment had been politics, not betrayal.

Tomorrow.

But tomorrow, Katie did not come.

William woke at sunset, and she was not waiting in the dining room. Not reading in the library. Not exploring the halls.

Frederick met him in the corridor.

"Katie," William said. "Where is she?"

"She woke early this morning. Shortly after dawn." Frederick's voice was careful. "The servants report she barely slept. She spent the day with her parents in their quarters. She retired just before sunset."

Just before he woke. Deliberately avoiding him.

"She is upset," Frederick said. "About the dinner."

"I know."

"Will you speak to her?"

"She does not wish to speak to me." William felt the pull in his chest, stronger now. Anxious. "I will give her time."

He walked to the dining room. His thoughts were heavy, scattered. How to fix this. What to say. Whether he had made a mistake by not defending her publicly, or whether public confrontation would have made things worse.

He pushed open the dining room door.

And stopped.

Clara Parker sat at the table. Alone. Her hands wrapped around a cup of tea. Her expression unreadable.

"Mrs. Parker," William said.

"Your Majesty." Clara set down her tea. "I think we need to talk."

20

Matters of the Heart

William stood in the doorway.

Clara Parker sat at the table with her hands wrapped around a cup of tea that had long gone cold. She looked tired. The kind of tired that came from worry, not lack of sleep.

"Mrs. Parker," he said again. "Is something wrong? Is Katie—"

"Katie is asleep. Or pretending to be." Clara gestured to the chair across from her. "Please. Sit."

William sat.

He was not accustomed to taking orders. He was a king. He had ruled for decades. But something in Clara's voice brooked no argument.

"I understand you have two hundred years on me," Clara said. Her tone was calm. Measured. "In most matters, I would defer to your experience. You have seen more than I could imagine. Lived through things I have only read about in books."

William waited.

"But when it comes to matters of the heart." Clara met his eyes. "I am far more advanced than you."

The words landed. William did not argue.

"I am sure what happened tonight was a misunderstanding," Clara continued. "I am sure you had reasons for what you did. Good reasons, perhaps. Reasons that make sense in your world, with your politics, with your centuries of experience."

"I did have reasons."

"I believe you. But it is not my place to hear them." Clara set down her tea. "I am not here for an explanation, William. I am here to give you advice. Mother to king. If you will hear it."

William inclined his head. "I will hear it."

"Katie does not come from your world. She does not understand your protocols. She does not know how your council works, who has power, who is jockeying for position. She has been here two weeks. She has learned your sleep schedule and the layout of your library. That is all."

William said nothing. He could feel the shape of what was coming.

"Tonight was your first real test," Clara said. "The first time your relationship met your responsibilities. And you failed."

The word sat between them. Failed. William had not heard it directed at him in a very long time.

"She is eighteen years old," Clara continued. "She sat at that table surrounded by creatures older than nations. She tried to contribute when you asked her to. And when that man dismissed her, she looked to you. She looked to see what you would do."

"I addressed it afterward. Privately. I made clear to him that—"

"She does not know that." Clara's voice was gentle but firm. "She knows only what she saw. And what she saw was you apologizing. Agreeing. Moving on as if what he said was acceptable."

William closed his eyes.

"You may have handled it correctly from a king's standpoint," Clara said. "I do not know enough about your politics to say. But from a relationship standpoint? You did not handle it at all. You left her alone in that room, feeling small, and you did nothing she could see."

The fire crackled. The castle was silent around them.

"Did you know," Clara said, "that as Katie was growing up, she watched you on television?"

William opened his eyes. "What?"

"When the schools taught children about vampires, they taught them about you. When Katie saw interviews, read articles, looked at photographs. It was you." Clara's expression softened. "When she saw a vampire for the first time, truly saw one, it was you. On a screen in our living room when she was five years old."

William did not know what to say.

"She has known your face for most of her life. Known your voice. Your words. She has thought about you without even realizing she was doing it." Clara paused. "You are not a stranger to her, William. You never were. And that is why tonight hurt so much."

The weight of it settled over him. Thirteen years. She had been watching him for thirteen years. Learning him. Forming impressions he had never known about.

"Katie is strong," Clara said. "She has had to be. Life has not been easy for her. It takes a great deal to upset her." She leaned forward slightly. "She is angry at your council member. That man who dismissed her. She is furious with him."

"And with me?"

"No." Clara shook her head. "She is not angry with you. She is upset. There is a difference."

William frowned. "I do not understand."

"Anger comes from violation. From boundaries crossed. From wrongs that demand response." Clara's voice was quiet. "Upset comes from disappointment. From expectations unmet. From caring about someone and being hurt by them."

She let that sit.

"Can a person be upset," Clara asked, "if they do not care about the other person?"

William stared at her.

"She is still here," Clara said. "She did not pack her bags. She did not demand to leave. She is in her room, avoiding you, because she does not know how to feel. Because you matter to her, and she does not know what to do with that."

The pull in William's chest shifted. Changed. He had thought it was anxiety. Distance. But perhaps it was something else.

"I have said what I came to say." Clara stood. "The rest is between you and my daughter. I cannot fix it for you. I can only tell you that it is fixable, if you are willing to do the work."

"Mrs. Parker." William stood as well. "Thank you."

"Do not thank me yet. Thank me when you have made this right." She moved toward the door. Paused. "And William?"

"Yes?"

"She is eighteen. She has never been in a relationship. She does not know how to fight, how to forgive, how to navigate disappointment with someone she cares about." Clara's eyes were kind. "Be patient with her. She is learning. You both are."

She left.

William stood alone in the dining room.

The fire had burned low. The windows showed only darkness. The castle was quiet in the way it always was at this hour, caught between worlds.

Clara's words echoed in his mind. Katie had watched him. Known him. For thirteen years, he had been a face on a screen, a voice in interviews, a figure in her education. And he had not known.

He had thought of the waiting as one-sided. His burden to carry. His patience to maintain. He had not considered that she might have been waiting too. In her own way. Without even knowing what she was waiting for.

And tonight, he had let her down.

He understood now. The politics did not matter. The reasons did not matter. What mattered was what she had seen. What she had felt. The moment when she looked to him for protection and found only silence.

He had failed the first test. Clara was right.

But she was also right about something else. Katie was still here. She had not left. She was upset, not angry. Hurt, not finished.

That meant there was still something to save.

William walked to his study. The fire had gone out there too. He did not bother to relight it. He sat at his desk in the darkness and thought about what to do.

Words. He needed words. But not spoken ones. Not yet. She was not ready to hear him. She needed time. Space.

She needed to understand.

He reached for paper and began to write.

Katie,

I am writing this because I do not know if you will let me speak to you. Because words on paper can wait in ways that spoken words cannot. Because I owe you an explanation, and I want you to have it whether or not you choose to hear it from my voice.

What happened at the dinner was my failure. Not Samuel's. Mine.

I should have defended you. In that moment, in front of everyone, I should have made clear that you are not a little girl. That your voice matters. That dismissing you is not acceptable.

I did not do that. I chose politics over protection. I thought I was being strategic. I thought I would handle it privately, preserve appearances, maintain the careful balance of the council.

I was wrong.

You looked at me, Katie. I saw it. You looked at me to see what I would do. And I did nothing you could see. I left you alone in that room, surrounded by creatures who have forgotten what it means to be young, and I gave you silence when you needed support.

I am sorry. Those words are not enough, but they are true.

After you left, I found Samuel. I told him that you are to be Queen Consort. That you deserve respect. That it will not happen again. But that conversation happened in a corridor, out of your sight, and it does not undo what you felt in that dining hall.

I have ruled for decades. I have negotiated with nations. I have built systems that will outlast everyone currently alive. But I have never done this. I have never had someone to protect in the way that I want to protect you. And when the moment came, I chose wrong.

I am still learning. That is not an excuse. It is simply the truth.

Your mother came to see me tonight. She is wiser than I am in matters of the heart. She told me that you are upset, not angry. That there is a difference. That being upset means you care.

I hope that is true. I hope I have not broken something that cannot be repaired.

There is something else I want you to have. Something I have been keeping for eighteen years.

When you were born, I began writing letters. One each year on your birthday. I did not know if you would ever read them. I did not know if we would ever meet. But I needed to mark the time. To acknowledge that you existed. To speak to you even when speaking was impossible.

I am giving them to you now. All of them. Not because I expect anything in return. But because you deserve to know that you were never forgotten. That every year of your life, someone was thinking of you. Waiting for you. Hoping that one day, you would be exactly where you are now.

Read them or do not read them. That choice is yours. Everything is yours. It always has been.

I will be here when you are ready. However long that takes.

William

He set down the pen.

The ink dried slowly in the darkness. He read the words again. They were not perfect. They were not enough.

But they were honest. That would have to be sufficient.

He stood. Walked to the cabinet where he kept the things that mattered. The drawer that had been filling for eighteen years.

Eighteen envelopes. Each one marked with a year. Each one sealed with wax, waiting for a reader who might never come.

He gathered them carefully. Tied them with a ribbon he found in his desk. Dark blue. The color of the dress she had worn that first night.

He added his new letter to the top of the stack.

The walk to her door was quiet. The family wing was dark. No sound from behind any of the doors.

He knelt. Placed the bundle on the floor. The letters she had never known about. The years she had never seen.

He did not knock. Did not announce himself. Simply left them there, waiting for morning.

Then he rose and walked back through the silent castle.

The pull remained. Constant. Patient. Aching now in a way it had not ached before.

She was upset. But she was still here.

That had to mean something.

William returned to his study and sat in the darkness until dawn.

21

Eighteen Years

Katie woke to grey morning light.

She had not slept well. The dinner played behind her eyes every time she closed them. Samuel's dismissal. William's silence. The walk back to her room that had felt endless.

She had cried. She was not proud of that. But she had cried, and then she had lain awake, and then somehow morning had come without her noticing.

She pulled herself out of bed. Her eyes were swollen. Her head ached. She needed water. Tea. Something to make her feel human again.

She opened her door.

And stopped.

A bundle sat on the floor. Envelopes tied with dark blue ribbon. A letter on top, unsealed, her name written across the front in handwriting she did not recognize.

Katie stared at it for a long moment.

Then she knelt. Picked it up. Carried it back inside.

She sat on her bed and opened the loose letter first.

Katie,

I am writing this because I do not know if you will let me speak to you...

She read it slowly. Every word. Every apology. Every explanation she had not known she needed.

He had defended her. After she left. He had found Samuel in the corridor and made clear that it would not happen again. That she deserved respect. That she would be queen.

She had not known.

Your mother came to see me tonight. She is wiser than I am in matters of the heart.

Katie closed her eyes. Of course her mother had gone to him. Of course she had.

There is something else I want you to have. Something I have been keeping for eighteen years.

She looked at the bundle. The ribbon. The stack of envelopes beneath.

Seventeen of them. Each one marked with a year.

When you were born, I began writing letters. One each year on your birthday.

Katie's hands were shaking.

She untied the ribbon. Spread the envelopes across her bed. Year One. Year Two. Year Three. All the way to Year Seventeen.

Seventeen years of letters she had never known existed.

She started at the beginning.

Year One

To the child who carries the echo of me,

You were born today.

I learned of it three hours ago, in a room that has not changed in two hundred years. The fire was low. The rain was falling. And a piece of paper told me that somewhere across an ocean, you had taken your first breath.

Katie read about his mother. About patience. About a fisherman waiting his whole life for a particular fish.

I do not remember how the story ended. I think I fell asleep before she finished it. Children do that.

She smiled despite herself. The image of a young William, human and mortal, falling asleep to his mother's stories. It made him real in a way nothing else had.

Year Two

To the child who carries the echo of me,

You are two years old today. I am told this is the age when humans begin to form memories. The age when the world starts to become permanent.

I wonder what your first memory will be. A face. A voice. The smell of something cooking in a kitchen. The feeling of arms holding you safe.

I will not be in any of those memories. I am a stranger to you, and I will remain one for sixteen more years. That is as it should be. But I find myself hoping, selfishly perhaps, that your early memories are happy ones. That the foundation of your life is built on warmth.

My earliest memory is my mother singing. I do not remember the song. Only her voice, and the way it made the world feel smaller. Safer. Contained.

I hope someone is singing to you.

Katie wiped her eyes. Kept reading.

Year Three

To the child who carries the echo of me,

Frederick asked me today why I write these letters. I did not have a good answer.

I told him it was a record. A way to mark the years. He looked at me with that ancient patience of his and said nothing, which is his way of saying he does not believe me.

The truth is simpler and more foolish. I write because it makes you real. Because putting words on paper is the only way I can reach toward you. Because somewhere in Pennsylvania, a three-year-old girl is learning to speak in full sentences, and I will never hear any of them.

This is not self-pity. It is simply fact. The distance between us is necessary. I believe that. I support that. But believing in something does not make it painless.

I hope you are learning good words. Kind words. Words that will serve you well when you are old enough to choose them carefully.

She read Year Four. Year Five. Year Six.

Each letter was different. Some were short, only a few lines. Some stretched across pages. Some were reflective, philosophical. Others were almost playful, as if he were talking to a friend he had not seen in too long.

Year Seven

To the child who carries the echo of me,

I attended a human wedding today. A diplomatic function. The kind of thing I do because it maintains relationships, not because I enjoy it.

But I found myself watching the ceremony with unexpected attention. The vows. The rings. The way the couple looked at each other as if no one else existed.

Vampires do not have weddings. We have the bond, which is deeper and more permanent than any human ceremony. But we do not have the celebration. The public declaration. The moment when two people stand before everyone they love and say, "This is my choice. This is my future."

I wonder sometimes if we have lost something in that. If the privacy of our bonds has cost us the joy of proclamation.

If you and I ever stand together, I think I would like there to be witnesses. I think I would like the world to know.

But that is over ten years away, if it happens at all. For now, I simply watch other people's weddings and wonder what ours might look like.

Katie's chest ached.

She kept reading.

Year Ten

To the child who carries the echo of me,

You are ten years old today. Double digits, as humans say. A milestone.

I have been thinking about milestones. The way humans mark time with celebrations and ceremonies. Birthdays. Graduations. Anniversaries. Each one a flag planted in the soil of existence, saying "I was here. I made it this far."

Vampires do not do this. When you have lived for centuries, individual years lose their meaning. They blur together. One decade becomes indistinguishable from the next.

But I have been counting your years. Every single one. And I find that they do not blur at all. Each one is distinct. Precious. A year closer to knowing you.

Ten years. Eight more to go.

I am halfway there.

Year Twelve made her cry.

This month I learned that a girl died.

She was fourteen. Her name does not matter here... She was killed in an accident. A car on a wet road. Nothing dramatic. Nothing that would make history. Just a moment of inattention, and a life ended before it had properly begun.

He had been afraid. All those years. Afraid that something would happen to her before they could meet. Afraid that the waiting would be for nothing.

If you are reading this someday, it will mean that you survived the years I could not protect you from.

She had survived. She was here.

Year Thirteen. Year Fourteen.

Year Fourteen

To the child who carries the echo of me,

I made a mistake today.

Not a large one. A small failure of patience in a council meeting. A sharp word where a gentle one would have served better. The kind of thing I would not have noticed a century ago.

But I noticed it today. And I found myself wondering what you would think if you had seen it. Whether you would be disappointed. Whether you would understand.

This is new. This measuring of myself against an imaginary standard. This wondering how I appear through eyes that have never seen me.

I think perhaps it is making me better. The thought of you. The hope that someday I will have to be worthy of your attention.

Four more years. I am trying to use them well.

Year Fifteen. Year Sixteen.

Year Sixteen

To the child who carries the echo of me,

Two years.

I have started preparing. Not visibly. Not in ways anyone would notice. But in small ways. Quiet ways.

I have been learning about your country. Your region. The town where you grew up. I have studied maps and read histories and tried to under-stand the place that shaped you.

I know it is rural. Modest. The kind of place where people work hard and expect little. I know the economy is difficult. I know the winters are cold.

I do not know you. But I am trying to know the world that made you.

Two years. Soon I will have to stop imagining and start learning. I am not sure which is more terrifying.

Year Seventeen made her hands shake.

I am afraid.

There. I have written it. A king, afraid. Afraid of a meeting that may go badly. Afraid of hope that may prove unfounded. Afraid of finding, after all this waiting, that the connection means nothing.

He had been afraid of her. Of this. Of exactly what was happening right now.

I have prepared myself for rejection. I have rehearsed acceptance. I have told myself, again and again, that your choice is yours alone, and that I will respect it without complaint.

I am not certain I believe myself.

Katie sat on her bed surrounded by paper.

Windows into the mind of a man who had been waiting for her since before she could walk.

She thought about the dinner. About Samuel's dismissal. About William's silence.

She thought about what her mother must have said to him. About the letter he had written after. About the apology she had not been ready to hear.

He had failed. He had admitted that. But he had also been trying. For eighteen years, he had been trying to be someone she would want to know.

And she had almost thrown that away because of one bad moment.

Katie gathered the letters carefully. Stacked them. Tied them again with the blue ribbon.

She looked at the clock. Early afternoon. Hours until sunset. Hours until he would wake.

She could wait here. In her room. Let him come to her.

But that felt wrong. Passive. Like hiding from something she needed to face.

She stood. Washed her face. Changed her clothes. Gathered the letters and held them against her chest.

Then she walked to the library.

The castle was quiet around her. Daylight staff moved through the halls, nodding politely as she passed. She found her way without difficulty. The paths were familiar now.

The library was empty. Dust motes floated in the grey light from the windows. The fire was cold.

Katie found the chair where she had fallen asleep before. The one by the window. The one where he had woken her gently and asked if she was hungry.

She sat. Set the letters on the table beside her.

She would wait. However long it took.

The afternoon stretched. The light shifted. Katie watched the shadows move across the floor and thought about everything she had read. Every word. Every year.

She had known he was waiting. She had not understood what that meant.

Two hundred years of solitude. Eighteen years of hope. Letters written to someone who might never read them.

He had loved her before he knew her. Not romantically. Not the way songs and stories described love. But in a quieter way. A more patient way. The love of someone who believes in a future they cannot see.

She thought about her anger. Her hurt. The way she had avoided him, hidden from him, refused to let him explain.

She had been right to be upset. But she had also been unfair.

The light began to fade. Gold to grey to something darker.

Katie's eyes grew heavy. She had not slept well the night before. The warmth of the library wrapped around her like a blanket.

She told herself she would just rest her eyes. Just for a moment.

She fell asleep with the letters beside her and William's words echoing in her mind.

William woke at sunset.

The pull was immediate. Stronger than usual. She was somewhere in the castle, and she was not hiding.

He dressed quickly. Followed the thread of awareness through the halls.

The library.

He found her in the chair by the window. Asleep. The letters stacked on the table beside her, the blue ribbon trailing across the wood.

She had read them. All of them.

William stood in the doorway and watched her breathe. The way her chest rose and fell. The way her hair fell across her face. The peaceful set of her features, so different from the hurt he had seen two nights ago.

She had come here to wait for him. She had read his words and decided to stay.

He crossed to her chair. Knelt beside it. Reached out and touched her shoulder.

"Katie."

She stirred. Her eyes opened slowly. Confusion first, then recognition.

"William." Her voice was rough with sleep. "What time is it?"

"Just past sunset." He did not move from his crouch. Did not presume to stand over her. "You fell asleep."

"I was waiting for you." She sat up. Rubbed her eyes. "I read the letters."

"I know."

"All of them."

"I hoped you would."

She looked at him. Her eyes were red. From sleep, perhaps. Or from crying. He could not tell.

"I'm sorry," she said.

William blinked. "You are sorry?"

"For avoiding you. For not letting you explain. For assuming the worst without giving you a chance." She shook her head. "I was hurt, and I handled it badly. That wasn't fair to you."

"Katie." He reached for her hand. Stopped himself. Let his hand fall. "You have nothing to apologize for. I failed you. In front of everyone. I let that man dismiss you and I said nothing."

"You said something after. I read your letter. You told him—"

"After is not enough. You needed me in that moment, and I was not there." William's voice was quiet. "I have ruled for decades. I have navigated politics more complicated than anything that council has produced. And I still chose wrong. I chose strategy over you."

"You didn't know what I needed. I didn't tell you."

"You should not have had to tell me." He shook his head. "I am two hundred years old. I have watched humans my entire existence. I should have known. I should have seen your face and understood."

They sat in silence. The library darkened around them. The last light faded from the windows.

"Your letters," Katie said finally. "The one from Year Seventeen. You said you were afraid."

"I was. I am."

"Of what? Of me saying no?"

"Of everything." William met her eyes. "Of the moment you look at me and decide I am not what you want. Of failing you in ways I cannot predict. Of being so old and so set in my ways that I cannot learn to be what you need."

"You're learning now."

"Am I?" His voice was rough. "It does not feel like learning. It feels like stumbling. Making mistakes. Hoping you will forgive them."

"That is learning." Katie reached out. Touched his hand where it rested on the arm of her chair. "That's exactly what learning feels like."

William looked at her hand on his. Her warmth against his cold skin.

"I should have defended you," he said. "In front of everyone. I should have made clear that you matter. That your voice matters. That anyone who dismisses you dismisses me as well."

"Yes. You should have."

"I will not make that mistake again."

"I know." She squeezed his hand. "I believe you."

They sat together in the darkness. The fire was cold. The windows showed only stars.

"I read the letter about the girl who died," Katie said quietly. "The one from Year Twelve."

William nodded. He remembered writing it. The grief that was not quite his. The fear that lived beneath it.

"You were afraid that would happen to me."

"Every year. Every day, if I am honest." He turned his hand over. Let her fingers rest in his palm. "The waiting was not passive. It was terrified. Every time I thought of you, I thought of all the ways I could lose you before we ever met."

"But you didn't lose me."

"No. I did not."

Katie was quiet for a moment.

"I watched you," she said. "When I was growing up. On television. In articles. My mom told you that."

"She did."

"I didn't know it was you I was watching. I didn't know about the mark. But I remember thinking you seemed different from what I expected. From what the stories said vampires would be." She paused. "You seemed sad."

William considered that. "I probably was."

"Are you still?"

He looked at her. At the letters on the table. At the hand resting in his.

"Less," he said. "Less than I was."

Katie smiled. It was small. Tentative. But real.

"I want to keep trying," she said. "The month. The courtship. All of it. I want to see where this goes."

"Even after what happened?"

"Especially after what happened." She squeezed his hand again. "You made a mistake. You owned it. You apologized. That matters more than the mistake."

William felt something loosen in his chest. Something that had been tight since the dinner. Since before the dinner, if he was honest. Since he first learned that she existed and realized how many ways he could fail her.

"Thank you," he said.

"Don't thank me yet." Katie's smile widened slightly. "Thank me when we've made it through the whole month without any more disasters."

"I will do my best."

"That's all I'm asking." She stood. Stretched. Her joints cracked in the quiet. "Now. I've been sleeping in chairs for hours and I'm starving. Is there any chance of dinner?"

William stood as well. He found himself smiling. Something he had not done since before the council meeting.

"I believe that can be arranged."

They walked out of the library together. The castle was quiet around them. The halls were dark, lit only by the occasional lamp.

Katie carried the letters with her. Held them against her chest like something precious.

Eighteen years of words. Eighteen years of waiting.

And now, finally, the chance to see what came next.

22

What Forever Looks Like

The gardens were different at night.

Katie had seen them from windows. During the day, they were beautiful in a quiet, Scottish way. Hedges and stone paths. Flower beds that had been tended for centuries. A fountain that did not work anymore but remained because removing it would have been a kind of betrayal.

But at night, with the lights, they became something else entirely.

"When did you do all this?" Katie asked.

They walked side by side along a gravel path. Lanterns hung from iron posts, casting pools of warm light across the stones. Strings of smaller lights wound through the hedges, creating constellations in the darkness. The air was cold but still. No wind tonight.

"The lights have been here for decades," William said. "My mother loved the gardens. My father had them illuminated so she could walk with him after dark."

"That's romantic."

"He was a romantic. Though he would have denied it fiercely." William smiled slightly. "He once told me that romance was simply paying attention. Noticing what someone loved and finding ways to give it to them."

Katie considered that. "That's a good definition."

"I thought so. I have been trying to live by it."

They walked in comfortable silence. The castle rose behind them, windows glowing. Somewhere in the distance, an owl called.

"Can I ask you something?" Katie said.

"You can always ask me something."

"Your speed. Your strength. The things vampires can do." She glanced at him. "I've read about it. Seen it mentioned in articles. But I've never actually seen it."

"Would you like to?"

Katie nodded.

William stopped walking. He looked around the garden, assessing. Then he pointed to a stone bench perhaps fifty feet away, barely visible in the darkness beyond the lights.

"Watch the bench," he said.

Katie watched.

One moment he was beside her. The next, he was sitting on the bench, legs crossed, expression mild. She had not seen him move. There had been no blur, no rush of air. He had simply been in one place, and then another.

"That's terrifying," she said.

"I prefer impressive." He was beside her again. She still had not seen him move. "But I understand terrifying."

"How fast is that exactly?"

"Faster than any human can track. Faster than most cameras can capture." He resumed walking. She fell into step beside him. "It varies among vampires. Age increases speed, to a point. So does rest. So does the bond."

"The bond makes you faster?"

"The bond enhances everything. Speed. Strength. Senses. Bonded vampires are measurably more powerful than unbonded ones." He paused. "It is one of the reasons the Echo Mark is so valued. Beyond the emotional connection."

Katie filed that away. "What about strength? How strong are you?"

"Strong enough that I must be very careful." His voice was matter-of-fact. "I could lift this bench with one hand. I could tear through stone walls if I needed to. But I could also hurt someone without meaning to, if I forgot to restrain myself."

"Have you ever? Hurt someone by accident?"

"Once. When I was newly transformed. I did not yet understand my own body." Something flickered across his face. "I broke a man's arm by gripping it too tightly. I have not forgotten the sound."

They walked in silence for a moment.

"If we bonded," Katie said slowly, "would I have any of that? The speed? The strength?"

"Not to the same degree. But yes, some." William guided her around a corner in the path. A new section of garden opened before them, this one with roses climbing ancient trellises. "Bonded humans gain enhanced reflexes. Better healing. A resistance to illness and injury that goes beyond normal."

"And the longevity."

"And the longevity." He nodded. "Two to three times the normal human lifespan, typically. Some longer."

"So I could live to be two hundred?"

"Possibly. Perhaps longer." He glanced at her. "Does that frighten you?"

Katie thought about it. Really thought about it, not just the knee-jerk reaction.

"A little," she admitted. "Not the living part. The watching part. Everyone I know would die. My parents. Friends. Everyone from my old life."

"Yes. That is the cost." His voice was gentle. "It is not a small thing. I would never pretend otherwise."

"But I'd have you."

"You would have me. For as long as you wanted me."

They reached a stone bench. A different one, nestled in an alcove surrounded by roses. Katie sat. William sat beside her, careful to leave space between them.

"Can we talk about it?" Katie asked. "What it would actually look like? If I stayed?"

"Of course."

"The Queen Consort thing. What does that actually mean?"

William leaned back. Considered the question.

"It means you would rule beside me. Not in name only. In practice." He paused. "My mother never took the formal role. She and my father did not complete the bond, and she preferred to remain private. But if you chose to bond with me, you would have authority. Real authority."

"Authority over what?"

"Over vampires. Over our laws and customs and conflicts." He turned to face her. "I am not like a human king, Katie. I do not rule a country. I rule a species. Every vampire on Earth, regardless of where they live, falls under my authority."

Katie stared at him. She had known this, intellectually. But hearing it stated plainly was different.

"How many vampires are there?"

"Approximately fifty thousand worldwide. The number fluctuates. We do not reproduce quickly, and we lose members occasionally to violence or accident."

"Fifty thousand." She tried to grasp it. "And you're responsible for all of them?"

"For their governance, yes. For resolving disputes. For maintaining the peace with human governments. For ensuring the Accord is honored." He smiled slightly. "It is a great deal of work. Frederick handles most of the day-to-day matters. But the decisions fall to me."

"And they would fall to me too? If I became Queen Consort?"

"In time. You would need to learn first. Our history. Our laws. The relationships between different factions and families." He paused. "It is not something that happens overnight. My mother spent fifty years learning, and she never felt she had mastered it."

Katie nodded slowly. The scope of it was overwhelming. But somehow, sitting here in this garden with the lights around them, it felt manageable. Distant enough to consider without panic.

"What else would I need to learn?"

"Languages, ideally. English is sufficient for most purposes, but many of our older vampires prefer their native tongues. French. German. Spanish. Mandarin, increasingly." He ticked them off. "You would not need fluency. But enough to show respect. To demonstrate that you are trying."

"I took Spanish in high school. I was terrible at it."

"You would have excellent tutors. And decades to practice." His eyes crinkled slightly. "Vampires are patient teachers. We have learned that rushing humans rarely produces good results."

Katie laughed. "That's reassuring."

They sat in comfortable silence. The roses rustled in a faint breeze. The lights glowed steady and warm.

"What about travel?" Katie asked. "You said you rule vampires everywhere. Does that mean we'd have to go places?"

"Regularly. The Americas. Europe. Asia. Africa. Anywhere our people live, we are expected to visit periodically." William paused. "It can be exhausting. But it can also be wonderful. There are places in this world that most humans never see. Ancient sites. Hidden communities. Beauty that has been preserved for centuries."

"And I'd see all of that?"

"If you wanted to. The world would open to you, Katie. Not just geographically. In every way." He turned to face her fully. "I know this is overwhelming. I know it sounds like a fantasy, or perhaps a nightmare, depending on your perspective. But I want you to understand what I am offering. Not just me. Not just the bond. A life larger than anything you might have imagined."

Katie looked at him. At the lights reflected in his dark eyes. At the careful stillness of his body, the restraint she was beginning to recognize as fundamental to who he was.

"What if I'm not good at it?" she asked quietly. "What if I try to be Queen Consort and I fail?"

"Then we learn from the failure and try again." His voice was calm. Certain. "Katie, I have ruled for decades. I have made mistakes that cost lives. I have failed in ways I still carry with me. Leadership is not about perfection. It is about persistence."

"That sounds exhausting."

"It is. But it is also meaningful." He reached out. Took her hand. His skin was cool against hers. "You would not be alone. You would have me. You would have advisors and teachers and an entire structure built to support you. And you would have time. More time than you can currently imagine."

Katie looked at their joined hands. His pale. Hers warm. The contrast was stark.

"Can you feel that?" she asked. "My warmth?"

"Yes. You are very warm to me." He paused. "When the bond is complete, I am told it changes. That mates feel normal to each other. Neither warm nor cold. Simply right."

"Simply right."

"That is how it was described to me."

Katie smiled. "That sounds nice."

"I have been hoping it is."

They sat together as the night deepened. The garden lights glowed. The roses released their fragrance into the cool air.

"Tell me about the places," Katie said. "The ones you mentioned. The ancient sites. The hidden communities."

William smiled. And he told her.

He told her about a monastery in Tibet where vampires had lived for a thousand years, studying philosophy and preserving texts that existed nowhere else. About a city beneath Rome, built in the catacombs, where the oldest vampires in Europe gathered once a decade to debate and drink and remember. About islands in the Pacific that appeared on no human map, maintained as sanctuaries for those who wanted to withdraw from the world.

He told her about the aurora borealis seen from a mountain in Norway where no human had ever stood. About libraries in Alexandria that had survived when the famous one burned. About a garden in Japan that had been tended by the same vampire for eight hundred years.

Katie listened. Asked questions. Laughed at the funny parts and went quiet at the sad ones.

The night stretched on. Neither of them noticed.

"We should go in," William said finally. The sky was beginning to lighten at the edges. "Dawn approaches."

"Already?" Katie looked up. She had lost track of time entirely. "I'm not tired."

"You will be. Your body is still adjusting to our schedule." He stood. Offered her his hand. "Come. I will walk you back."

They walked through the garden together. The lights were beginning to dim, preparing for the sunrise that would make them unnecessary.

"William?" Katie said as they reached the castle doors.

"Yes?"

"Thank you. For tonight. For telling me all of that." She squeezed his hand. "For making it seem possible instead of terrifying."

"It is possible. All of it." He opened the door for her. "The question is simply whether you want it."

Katie stepped inside. Turned to face him.

"I'm starting to think I might," she said.

Something shifted in his expression. Hope, maybe. Or the beginning of belief.

"That is more than I dared to expect," he said quietly.

"Get used to it." She smiled. "I'm full of surprises."

"I am beginning to realize that too."

She walked toward her quarters. He watched her go, standing in the doorway as the first light of dawn crept across the floor.

One more week. One more week to convince her. To show her what their life could be.

He had never wanted anything more.

23

The Final Week

Seven days.

Katie stood at her window and watched the sun set over the Highlands. The sky was painted in shades of orange and gold, the kind of sunset that belonged in paintings. In a week, she would either be watching it from this same window or from a plane heading home.

A knock at her door.

"Come in."

William entered. He moved carefully, the way he always did. Conscious of space. Conscious of not overwhelming.

"May I speak with you?" he asked.

"Of course."

He did not sit. He stood near the door, hands clasped behind his back. Something about his posture was different tonight. More formal. More restrained.

"This is your final week," he said. "In seven days, you will need to make a decision."

"I know."

"I want to be clear about something." He met her eyes. "I do not want to influence that decision. Not through pressure. Not through expectation. Not through the weight of everything I have shown you."

Katie frowned. "What are you saying?"

"I am saying that I am going to step back. This week, I will not seek you out. I will not fill your evenings with conversation and gardens and demonstrations of what our life could be." He paused. "If you want to see me, you know where to find me. But the seeking should be yours."

"You're pulling away?"

"I am giving you space." His voice was gentle. "You have spent three weeks learning who I am. Now you need time to decide what that means to you. Without me standing beside you, hoping."

Katie wanted to argue. Wanted to tell him that his presence was not pressure, that she liked having him near. But she understood what he was doing. Why he was doing it.

"There are people you should talk to," William continued. "Your parents, obviously. But also the registry representatives. Eleanor and Elise. They can explain what happens either way. What your life looks like if you stay. What it looks like if you go."

"You want me to talk to them?"

"I want you to have all the information. Every perspective. Not just mine." He moved toward the door. "This decision will shape the rest of your life, Katie. However long that life turns out to be. I will not have you make it without understanding the full weight of what you are choosing."

He paused at the threshold.

"If you have questions, I am here. Always. But I will not come to you. Not this week." Something flickered in his eyes. Something that looked like it cost him. "Seek me out when you are ready. Or do not. Either way, I will accept your choice."

Then he was gone.

Katie stood in the empty room and felt the silence settle around her.

She talked to her parents first.

They sat in the conservatory the next morning. Rain streaked the glass. Tea grew cold on the table between them.

"What do you want to do?" Clara asked.

"I don't know. That's the problem."

"No." Clara shook her head. "That's not what I asked. I asked what you want. Not what makes sense. Not what seems right. What do you actually want?"

Katie looked at her mother. At the lines around her eyes that had not been there a year ago. At the grey in her hair that seemed to have multiplied since they arrived.

"I think I want to stay," she said quietly.

"Then stay."

"It's not that simple."

"Why not?"

Katie did not have a good answer.

Thomas had been quiet through the conversation. Now he leaned forward.

"When your mother and I got married," he said, "everyone told us it was a mistake. We were too young. Too poor. Too different from what each other's families expected." He paused. "We did it anyway. Because we knew. We just knew."

"How?" Katie asked. "How did you know?"

"I can't explain it. It was just there. This certainty." Thomas looked at Clara. Something passed between them. Twenty years of history in a single glance. "When you know, you know. The question is whether you know."

Katie thought about William. About the letters. About three weeks of conversations and chess games and walks through illuminated gardens.

Did she know?

She was not sure. But she was starting to think she might.

Eleanor and Elise came to the castle early that evening.

They sat in the same room where Katie had first met them. The same table. The same chairs. But everything felt different now. Three weeks had passed. Katie was not the same person who had signed those papers.

"You wanted to speak with us," Eleanor said. "About your options."

"I want to understand what happens either way."

Eleanor nodded. She pulled out a folder. Different papers this time. Different documents.

"If you choose to leave," she said, "you return home. The courtship ends. The match remains on record, but no further action is taken. His Majesty has already arranged financial support for your family. That continues regardless of your decision."

"He told me that."

"I wanted to confirm it officially." Eleanor set aside the first paper. "You would be free to live your life as you choose. Marry someone else, if you wished. Have children. Pursue whatever future appeals to you."

Katie nodded. She had known all of this.

"If you choose to stay," Eleanor continued, "the courtship transitions to a bonding period. This is more formal. There are ceremonies. Rituals. The exchange."

"The blood."

"Yes. The bond cannot be completed without it." Eleanor's voice was matter-of-fact. "After the bond, you would officially become Queen Consort. You would have duties. Responsibilities. A role in vampire governance that would expand over time."

Elise spoke for the first time. "You would also have protections. Legal status that extends to every nation where the Accord is honored. Resources. Support. A life that most humans cannot imagine."

"And I could never leave."

"The bond is permanent," Elise confirmed. "Once completed, it cannot be undone. You would be tied to His Majesty for as long as you both exist."

Katie sat with that. The weight of forever. The impossibility of changing her mind.

"What do most people do?" she asked. "The other Echo Mark matches. Do they usually bond?"

Eleanor and Elise exchanged glances.

"Most do," Eleanor said carefully. "The match is rare. Those who find it tend to value it. But there have been cases where humans chose to walk away. It is not common, but it happens."

"And the vampires? The ones whose matches left?"

"They survive." Elise's voice was quiet. "It is painful. The pull does not disappear simply because the human rejects it. But they survive. They continue. They find meaning in other things."

Katie thought about William. About what it would cost him if she left. About the two hundred years he had waited and the centuries he would continue to wait, alone.

"Can I ask you something?" she said. "Both of you. Honestly."

"Of course," Eleanor said.

"If you were me. If you were eighteen years old and facing this choice. What would you do?"

The room was silent.

"I cannot answer that," Eleanor said finally. "It would not be appropriate."

"I can." Elise's voice cut through. Eleanor shot her a look, but Elise ignored it. "If I were you. If I were eighteen and human and had a king waiting for me. A king who had built systems to find me. Who had shown the patience and restraint that William has shown." She paused. "I would stay. Without question."

Eleanor sighed. "Elise."

"She asked. She deserves an honest answer." Elise met Katie's eyes. "I have known William for two centuries. He is not perfect. He makes mistakes. But he is good, in a way that is rare among our kind. He will protect you. He will value you. He will spend every day of your life trying to be worthy of you."

Katie felt something shift in her chest.

"Thank you," she said. "For being honest."

Elise inclined her head. "Whatever you decide, you have my respect. This is not an easy choice. But you are facing it with more grace than most would manage."

They left her alone after that. Katie sat in the empty room and thought about everything they had said.

That night, she read the letters again.

All eighteen of them. From Year One to Year Eighteen. She spread them across her bed and traced the words with her fingers. The handwriting that had become familiar. The voice that had become dear.

She lingered on Year Twelve. The letter about the girl who died.

If you are reading this someday, it will mean that you survived the years I could not protect you from.

She had survived. She was here. And now she had to decide whether to stay.

She thought about the question she had not yet asked. The doubt that still lingered in the back of her mind.

Tomorrow. She would find him tomorrow.

She found him in the library.

He was reading by the fire, a book open in his lap. He looked up when she entered but did not stand. Did not move toward her. Keeping his word about stepping back.

"Katie." His voice was careful. Neutral. "Is everything all right?"

"I have a question."

"Then ask."

She crossed the room. Sat in the chair across from his. The fire crackled between them.

"The Echo Mark," she said. "Is there any possibility it's wrong?"

William was silent for a moment. He closed his book. Set it aside.

"Wrong in what way?"

"That it's a mistake. That we're not actually matched. That this is all some kind of error and I'm not really your mate."

"No." His voice was certain. Absolute. "There is no error."

"How can you be sure?"

"Because the Echo Mark is only part of it." William leaned forward slightly. "The mark identifies. It tells us where to look. But it is not what confirms the bond. That confirmation comes from something else."

"What?"

"The pull." He met her eyes. "When a vampire finds their true mate, there is a physical sensation. A pull toward that person. It begins the moment we learn of the match and intensifies when we are near them. It cannot be faked. It cannot be manufactured. It simply is."

"And you feel that? With me?"

"From the moment I read the notification of your birth." His voice was quiet. "It has only grown stronger since you arrived. When you are near me, I am aware of you in a way I am aware of nothing else. When you are far, I can still feel where you are. The direction. The distance."

Katie absorbed this. "You always know where I am?"

"Always. It is not surveillance. I do not follow you. But I know." He paused. "If the mark were wrong, there would be no pull. There is a pull. Therefore, the mark is not wrong."

She sat with that. The certainty of it. The impossibility of doubt.

"Can I ask you something else?"

"Anything."

"Children." The word hung in the air between them. "If we bonded. If we stayed together. Could we have children?"

William's expression shifted. Something softer entered his eyes.

"Yes. Vampires can only reproduce with humans. It is one of the reasons the bond is so valued." He paused. "Any children we had would be born human. They would live as humans through childhood. And then, at puberty, the transformation would begin."

"They would become vampires?"

"By age twenty, yes. The process is gradual. It began for me when I was twelve and completed when I was twenty." He looked at the fire. "My mother watched me transform. She said it was strange, seeing her child become something she could never be. But she never regretted it. She said I was worth every moment of uncertainty."

Katie thought about that. About children who would outlive her. About watching them grow and change and become something she could not follow.

"Would I live long enough to see them transform?"

"With the bond? Yes. You would have decades with them. Centuries, perhaps." William's voice was gentle. "You would not miss their lives, Katie. You would be there for all of it."

She nodded slowly. Another piece falling into place.

"I should go," she said. "I need to think."

"Of course." William did not try to stop her. Did not ask what she was thinking. He simply watched her stand and walk toward the door.

"William?"

"Yes?"

"Thank you. For giving me space. For not pushing."

"I told you I would not."

"I know. But it must be hard. Waiting. Not knowing what I'll decide."

Something flickered across his face. Pain, maybe. Or hope held too tightly.

"I have waited over two hundred years," he said quietly. "I can wait seven more days."

She left him there, alone with his book and his fire and his endless patience.

The days passed.

Katie walked the gardens alone. Read in the library alone. Ate meals with her parents and talked about everything except the choice she was trying to make.

She thought about home. About the house with the leaky roof. About the friends she had left behind. About the future she had imagined before any of this happened.

She thought about William. About the letters. About the gardens and the chess games and the conversations that had stretched into dawn.

She thought about forever. About what it meant to choose someone for eternity. About the weight of a decision that could not be undone.

On the sixth night, she found herself in front of his study door.

She did not knock. She stood there, hand raised, heart pounding.

What was she waiting for? What more did she need to know?

She had talked to her parents. She had talked to the representatives. She had read the letters until she could recite them from memory.

She knew what she wanted. She had known for days.

She was just afraid to say it out loud.

The door opened.

William stood there, surprise flickering across his face. He had not expected her.

"Katie."

"I'm ready," she said.

He stepped back. Let her enter. The study was warm, fire burning low, books scattered across the desk. The room of a man who had been trying to distract himself from waiting.

"Ready for what?" he asked.

"To decide."

He went still. Completely, utterly still in the way only vampires could manage.

"You do not have to decide tonight. You have one more day."

"I don't need one more day." Katie moved to the center of the room. Turned to face him. "I've spent a week thinking. Talking. Reading your letters until I could recite them. I know what I want."

William did not speak. He barely seemed to breathe.

"I'm scared," Katie said. "I want you to know that. I'm terrified. This is the biggest decision I've ever made and I can't undo it and part of me wants to run away and pretend none of this ever happened."

Still, he said nothing. Just watched her with those dark eyes that had seen two centuries pass.

"But I'm also sure." Her voice steadied. "When I think about going home. About living the life I would have lived if you'd never found me. It feels small. Empty. Like trying to fit back into clothes I've outgrown."

"Katie."

"Let me finish." She took a breath. "When I think about staying. About learning to be Queen Consort. About centuries with you, watching the world change, building something that matters. It's terrifying. But it's also right. It feels right in a way nothing else ever has."

She stepped closer to him. Close enough to see the firelight reflected in his eyes.

"You waited more than two hundred years," she said. "You wrote me letters, You built systems to find me and rules to protect me and you did all of it without any guarantee that I would want you back."

"I had to try." His voice was rough. "You were worth trying for."

"I know." She reached out. Took his hands. His skin was cool against hers. "That's why I'm choosing you."

Something shattered behind his eyes. The careful control he always maintained. The patience he had built over centuries.

"Katie." Her name was a prayer in his mouth.

"I consent to be your mate."

The words hung in the air between them. Final. Absolute. A choice that could never be unmade.

William closed his eyes. When he opened them again, they were wet.

"Say it again," he whispered.

Katie smiled. Felt tears on her own cheeks.

"I consent to be your mate."

He pulled her into his arms. Held her against his chest. His body was cool and solid and just right.

"Thank you," he said into her hair. "Thank you."

Katie held him back. Let herself be held.

She had made her choice.

Now it was time to see what came next.

24

Bound

The contract was simpler than Katie expected.

Three pages. Clear language. No hidden clauses or ancient formalities. Just a document stating that Kathryn Parker, of legal age and sound mind, consented to enter into a mate bond with William Stone, King of the Vampires.

She signed it at a desk in the great hall. The same hall William had shown her on her first tour. The thrones watched from the raised platform at the far end. Two of them, side by side.

Soon she would sit in one of them.

"Here," Eleanor said, pointing to a line at the bottom of the final page. "And here."

Katie signed. Her hand was steady. She had expected nerves, but instead she felt calm. Certain. The decision had already been made. This was just paperwork.

William signed beside her. His signature was precise, unhurried. He had waited over two centuries for this moment. He could afford to take his time with his name.

"Witnessed," Frederick said, adding his own signature. Elise signed as the second witness. Eleanor notarized the document with an official seal.

"It's done," Eleanor said. "Congratulations to you both."

Katie looked at William. He was looking at her. Something passed between them. Not joy, exactly. Something quieter. Relief, perhaps. The end of uncertainty.

"The photographers are ready," Frederick said. "Whenever you are prepared."

The photographs took longer than the signing.

They posed in the great hall first. Standing together near the thrones. Sitting at the desk where they had signed. William's hand on Katie's shoulder, formal and restrained.

Then they moved to the gardens. The lights were on despite the darkness. The same lights his father had installed for his mother. Katie thought about that as she smiled for the cameras. About history repeating itself. About love persisting across generations.

"One more," the photographer said. "Something less formal. More natural."

William glanced at Katie. She shrugged slightly.

He took her hand. Not posed. Just held it, the way he had held it a dozen times over the past month. The camera clicked.

"Perfect," the photographer said.

They reviewed the images afterward. Katie barely recognized herself. The girl in the photographs looked poised. Confident. Like someone who belonged in a castle beside a king.

"You photograph well," William said.

"I photograph terrified."

"Terrified looks good on you."

Katie laughed despite herself.

The broadcast aired the next evening.

They watched it together in a small sitting room. Katie's parents on one side of her, William on the other. The television showed images she had seen taken just hours before.

"His Majesty King William Stone has formally announced his mate bond," the newscaster said. "Kathryn Parker, eighteen, of Pennsylvania, was confirmed as his Echo Mark match one month ago. The pair signed the official bonding contract yesterday evening in a private ceremony at the royal residence."

The screen showed the photograph from the gardens. The one where William was holding her hand. Katie thought they looked happy. Nervous, but happy.

"Miss Parker is the first Queen Consort in over one hundred and forty years," the newscaster continued. "The previous consort, Margaret Stone, died in 1886. She and the late King Henry Stone were bonded for fifty-five years."

Katie watched her own face on the screen. Watched William's. The world was seeing them together for the first time. Judging. Wondering. Forming opinions about a relationship they knew nothing about.

"Sources close to the palace indicate that the bonding ceremony will take place in the coming days. Miss Parker is expected to assume her duties as Queen Consort following a period of transition and education."

The broadcast moved on to other news. Thomas muted the television.

"Well," he said. "That's that."

"That's that," Katie agreed.

The room was quiet. The weight of what had just happened settled over them. The world knew now. There was no going back.

"We need to talk," Clara said. "About what comes next."

They talked late into the morning.

Katie sat with her parents in their quarters. Tea grew cold. Dawn approached. But none of them moved to end the conversation.

"You could stay," Katie said. "There's room. More than enough room. You could live here."

Clara shook her head. "This isn't our world, sweetheart. We'd be in the way."

"You wouldn't be in the way."

"We would. Not intentionally. But we would." Clara reached over and took Katie's hand. "You're starting a new life. You need space to build it. Having your parents hovering won't help."

Thomas nodded slowly. "Your mother's right. We came here to make sure you were safe. You are. Now we need to let you grow."

Katie felt tears prick her eyes. "I don't want you to go."

"We're not disappearing. We're just going home." Clara squeezed her hand. "You'll visit. We'll visit. The king has already arranged it. Private flights whenever we want them."

"He did?"

"He asked us this morning. While you were with the photographers." Thomas's voice was rough. "Said family was important. Said he didn't want you to lose us just because you'd gained him."

Katie looked toward the door. Toward the hallway that led to William's chambers. He had done this quietly. Without telling her. Without asking for credit.

"We'll come back for the bonding celebration" Clara said. "And for holidays. And whenever you need us. This isn't goodbye, Katie. It's just... a new step."

Katie nodded. She understood. She hated it, but she understood.

"When will you leave?"

"Tomorrow evening. The king arranged transport." Clara smiled. "He's very good at arranging things."

"He is."

They sat together as the sun rose. Mother and daughter and father. A family that was changing shape but not ending.

"We're proud of you," Thomas said quietly. "Whatever happens. We're proud of who you are."

Katie leaned into him. Let herself be held the way she had been held as a child.

"I love you," she said.

"We love you too," Clara said. "Always."

The morning light filled the room. Outside, the world was waking up. Inside, a family said goodbye to what had been and hello to what would come.

Katie found William that evening.

He was in his study, reading by the fire. He looked up when she entered. Set aside his book.

"Your parents told me they've decided to return home," he said.

"They told me you arranged it. The flights. The visits." She sat in the chair across from him. "Thank you."

"They are your family. I meant what I said to your father. What is mine is yours. That includes the means to stay connected to the people you love."

Katie nodded. She looked at the fire. Gathered her thoughts.

"I need to talk to you about something."

"Of course."

"Us. What this means for us." She met his eyes. "I signed the contract. I consented to be your mate. But I'm still only eighteen. I've known you for a month. And I think..." She paused. "I think I'd like to take things slow."

William was quiet for a moment.

"Slow," he repeated.

"Yes. I'm not saying I regret my decision. I don't. But the romance part. The physical part. I need time with that." She felt her face heat. "Is that okay?"

"Katie." His voice was gentle. "You never need to ask if something is okay. Your pace is our pace. I have waited over two hundred years. I can wait as long as you need."

Relief flooded through her. "Really?"

"Really. I told you once that consent was sacred. That has not changed. It will never change." He paused. "However."

Katie tensed. "However?"

"There is something I would like to ask."

"What?"

"The bond ritual." William leaned forward slightly. "I know it sounds like the opposite of taking things slow. But I would like to complete it. Soon."

"Why?"

"Your safety." His voice was serious now. "You have consented to be my mate. The world knows it. That makes you a target. There are vampires who disagree with my policies. With the Accord. With everything I have built. If they wanted to hurt me, hurting you would be the most effective way to do it."

Katie felt cold. She had not thought about that.

"The bond offers protection," William continued. "Once it is complete, you will be stronger. Faster. Harder to hurt. Your body will heal more quickly. You will not be invulnerable, but you will be far more resilient than you are now."

"And the other part? The connection?"

"I will know if you are in danger. Immediately. No matter where you are." His eyes were intent. "Right now, I can feel the pull. I know you are nearby. But I cannot sense your wellbeing. If someone took you. If someone hurt you. I might not know until it was too late."

Katie understood. The weight of what he was asking. The reasons behind it.

"The blood," she said slowly. "I drink from you. You drink from me."

"Yes. It is a small amount. Less than a blood donation." He paused. "I will not lie to you. There will be some pain. But not from me. A bite from a mate does not hurt. What you might feel is the bond itself, settling into place. Some humans describe it as uncomfortable. Others describe it as overwhelming. But it passes. And afterward..."

"Afterward?"

"Afterward, you will be protected. Connected. Safe in a way you cannot be now."

Katie thought about it. The fear that still lingered. The strangeness of what he was describing.

But also the logic of it. The protection it offered. The connection it would create.

"Okay," she said.

William blinked. "Okay?"

"Yes. Let's do it. Tonight."

"Katie, you do not have to decide immediately. Take time. Think about—"

"I've been thinking about it since the first week. Since you explained what the bond required." She stood. "I'm scared. I won't pretend I'm not. But I trust you. And I want to be safe."

William rose as well. He moved toward her. Stopped a foot away.

"You are certain?"

"I'm certain."

Something shifted in his expression. The careful control he always maintained seemed to soften. Just slightly. Just enough for her to see what lay beneath.

"Then we will need privacy," he said. "And time. The bond should not be rushed."

He led her to a room she had not seen before.

It was small. Intimate. A fire burned low in the hearth. Candles flickered on surfaces she could not identify in the dim light. The air smelled of something sweet. Incense, maybe. Or flowers.

Katie looked around. The walls were stone. The floor was covered with thick rugs. Two chairs sat facing each other near the fire.

"Sit," William said. "Please."

She sat. He sat across from her. Their knees almost touched.

"We will take this slowly," he said. "Tell me if you need to stop. At any point. For any reason."

Katie nodded. Her heart was pounding.

"I will go first," William said. "You will drink from me. Then I will drink from you." He paused. "My blood will taste sweet. Like sugar water, I am told. Yours will taste like... you. Like everything I have been waiting for."

He raised his wrist to his mouth.

Katie watched, transfixed, as his teeth extended. Not dramatically. Just enough. Sharp points where flat teeth had been.

He bit into his own wrist.

The skin parted easily. Blood welled up, dark against his pale skin. He held his wrist out to her.

"Drink," he said.

Katie took his wrist in her hands. Looked at the blood. Looked at him.

Then she lowered her mouth to the wound.

The taste was immediate. Sweet, just as he had said. Like honey dissolved in water. Like something she had not known she was craving until this moment.

She drank. Not much. A few swallows. She could feel it spreading through her, warm and strange, settling into places she had not known existed.

"Enough," William said gently.

She pulled back. Watched as the wound on his wrist began to close. Healing already. Within seconds, there was no mark at all.

"Now you," he said.

Katie offered her wrist. Her hand was trembling.

William took it gently. Raised it to his lips. His eyes met hers.

"This will not hurt," he said. "I promise."

He bit.

She felt pressure. A strange intimacy. But no pain. Just the sensation of something being taken, and something being given in return.

He drank. His eyes closed. His expression shifted into something she had never seen. Reverence, maybe. Or completion.

It lasted only seconds. Then he pulled back. His tongue swept across the wound, and Katie watched in amazement as her own skin began to heal.

"It's done," William said.

Katie felt it then. The bond. Settling into place inside her. A presence that had not been there before. An awareness of him that went beyond sight or sound.

She could feel him. His relief. His joy. His profound, overwhelming gratitude.

"I can feel you," she whispered.

"And I can feel you." His voice was rough. "At last. After all this time. I can feel you."

He took her hands in his. They sat together in the candlelight, the fire warming them, the bond humming between them like a living thing.

Katie expected to feel different. Transformed. But she still felt like herself. Just... more. Like a door had opened that she had not known was closed.

"How do you feel?" William asked.

"Strange. But good." She squeezed his hands. "Your hands."

"What about them?"

"They're warm." She looked down at their intertwined fingers. "You're not cold anymore."

William smiled. Something in his face cracked open. Two hundred years of waiting, resolved in a single moment.

"To you," he said. "I am warm to you."

Katie smiled back. Felt tears on her cheeks.

She was bound. Connected. Safe.

And somehow, impossibly, she was home.

25

New Rooms

Katie woke to sunlight and the strangest sensation she had ever experienced.

She was not alone.

Not physically. The room was empty. But somewhere in the castle, in a chamber she had never entered, William was sleeping. And she could feel him.

It was not intrusive. Not like someone watching over her shoulder. More like a presence at the edge of her awareness. A warmth that had nothing to do with temperature. She knew, without knowing how she knew, that he was relaxed. Content. Happy in a way that seemed to radiate through the bond like light through a window.

She lay in bed for a long moment, exploring the sensation. Testing its edges. When she focused, she could sense the direction he was in. The rough distance. If she concentrated harder, she could almost feel his breathing. Slow and steady. The rhythm of deep sleep.

This was what he had meant. The connection. The knowing.

She understood now why he had wanted it so badly.

Katie pushed herself out of bed and crossed to the mirror.

She stopped.

The face looking back was hers. The same brown hair. The same blue eyes. But something was different. Subtle. Hard to name.

She looked closer.

Her skin seemed clearer. The faint shadows under her eyes that came from adjusting to a vampire's schedule were gone. Her features looked sharper somehow. More defined.

She stepped back. Looked at her whole body.

Stronger. That was the word. Not dramatically muscled. But the softness she had always carried seemed to have firmed. Her posture was straighter. Her limbs looked capable in a way they had not before.

She raised her hand. Flexed her fingers. Felt the power in them. Not vampire strength. But more than she had possessed yesterday.

And her vision. She had not noticed at first, but now she did. Everything was crisp. Clear. The texture of the stone walls. The individual threads in the tapestry across the room. Details she would have needed to squint to see before.

The bond had changed her. Physically. Already.

She wondered what else would change.

Breakfast was interrupted by chaos.

Katie was halfway through her eggs when the doors to the small dining room burst open and a woman swept in like a storm in human form.

"Miss Parker. Wonderful. We have so much to discuss."

The woman was perhaps fifty, impeccably dressed, with grey hair pulled back in a severe bun. Behind her trailed three assistants carrying folders, fabric samples, and what appeared to be an entire library of binders.

"I'm sorry," Katie said. "Who are you?"

"Julia Drake. Event coordination." The woman set a massive folder on the table, narrowly missing Katie's tea. "I've been retained to organize your bonding celebration. We have one month. That is not enough time, but we will manage."

Katie stared at her. "Bonding celebration?"

"The ball. The formal announcement. The ceremony where you are presented to vampire society as Queen Consort." Julia flipped open the folder. "Guest lists. Invitations. Catering. Decorations. Entertainment. Security. Protocol. We need decisions on all of it."

"I just woke up."

"And you are already behind schedule." Julia's tone was brisk but not unkind. "I understand this is overwhelming. But the world is watching, Miss Parker. Your first public appearance as Queen Consort will set the tone for everything that follows. We cannot afford to get it wrong."

Katie looked at her eggs. They were getting cold.

"Can I at least finish breakfast?"

Julia paused. Something like sympathy flickered across her face.

"Of course. My apologies." She stepped back. "I will wait in the drawing room. Join me when you are ready. But please. Do not take too long."

She swept out as dramatically as she had entered. Her assistants scurried behind her, leaving a trail of fabric samples in their wake.

Katie looked at her eggs again. Her appetite had vanished.

She ate them anyway. She had a feeling she was going to need the energy.

The morning was a blur of decisions.

Colours. Flowers. Music. Food. Guest lists that stretched into the hundreds. Protocol for greeting dignitaries. Protocol for the ceremony itself. Protocol for the reception afterward.

Katie's head spun. She said yes when she thought she should say yes. Said no when something felt wrong. Asked questions when she had no idea what was being discussed.

Julia was efficient. Patient, in her own brisk way. She explained things Katie did not understand. Offered options when Katie seemed lost. Made notes in a leather-bound book that never left her hand.

"The ceremony itself is simple," Julia said. "You and His Majesty will enter the great hall together. You will be formally introduced as Queen Consort. There will be speeches. A first dance. Then the reception begins."

"A first dance," Katie repeated.

"Yes. Do you know how to waltz?"

Katie thought about the dances at her high school. The awkward swaying that passed for slow dancing. "Not exactly."

"We will arrange lessons." Julia made a note. "Four weeks should be sufficient. You need not be expert. Simply competent."

Simply competent. Katie filed that away as the theme of her new life.

Her parents left that afternoon.

Katie stood in the courtyard and watched the car that would take them to the airfield. The sun was still up. William was still asleep. She had to say goodbye alone.

"Call us when you land," she said. "So I know you're safe."

"We will." Clara pulled her into a hug. Held her tight. "Take care of yourself, Katie. And let him take care of you too."

"I will."

Thomas hugged her next. He did not speak. Just held her for a long moment, his hand on the back of her head the way he had held her when she was small.

"I love you, Dad."

"I love you too, sweetheart." His voice was rough. "Be happy. That's all I ask."

They climbed into the car. Katie watched it drive away. Watched it disappear around the bend in the road. Watched until there was nothing left to see.

Then she went back inside and cried for an hour.

William found her in the library at sunset.

She had dried her tears by then. Had composed herself. Had settled into a chair by the fire with a book she was not reading.

But he knew anyway. She could feel his concern through the bond the moment he entered the room.

"Your parents left," he said.

"This afternoon. While you were sleeping."

"I am sorry I could not be there."

"It's okay. The sun was up." She set aside her book. "I said goodbye. They promised to call when they land."

William crossed to her. Sat in the chair across from hers. The same chairs where they had played chess. Where they had talked for hours.

"How are you feeling?" he asked. "Physically?"

Katie considered the question. "Different. Good different, I think. I noticed changes this morning."

"What kind of changes?"

"My vision is sharper. Everything looks clearer. And my body feels..." She searched for the right word. "Stronger. More defined. I looked in the mirror and I looked like someone who actually exercises."

William smiled slightly. "The bond enhances physical capabilities. It will continue over the coming weeks. The changes are more dramatic at first, then they slow."

"What else will change?"

"Your reflexes will improve. Your stamina. Your resistance to illness and injury." He paused. "You may also notice heightened senses. Better hearing. Better smell. Not to vampire levels, but beyond what humans typically experience."

Katie nodded. She had expected as much. But hearing it confirmed was still strange.

"I could feel you," she said. "This morning. While you were sleeping. I knew you were relaxed. Happy."

Something softened in William's expression. "I felt you too. The moment I woke. I knew where you were. I knew you had been crying."

"I was fine."

"I know. Crying does not mean you are not fine. It means you are processing." He leaned forward slightly. "I also felt when your parents left. The shift in your emotions. I wanted to come to you, but the sun..."

"I understand. I do." She reached out. Took his hand. His skin was warm against hers. Still strange, after weeks of cold. "It's going to take some getting used to. Feeling each other like this."

"Yes. But I find I prefer it to the alternative."

"What's the alternative?"

"Not feeling you at all." His thumb traced circles on her palm. "I spent two hundred years with silence where you should have been. Now you are there. I would not trade that for anything."

Katie felt her chest tighten. In a good way. The best way.

"I met Julia Drake today," she said. "The event coordinator."

"Ah." Something flickered across William's face. Amusement, maybe. "She is... efficient."

"That's one word for it. She told me I need to learn to waltz."

"You do not know how to waltz?"

"I went to a public high school in rural Pennsylvania. We swayed. Sometimes in rhythm."

William laughed. A real laugh. The kind she had only heard a few times before.

"I will teach you," he said. "If you would like. I have had several centuries to perfect the art."

"Several centuries of waltzing. That sounds incredibly boring."

"It was not always waltzing. Dance styles change. I have learned most of them over the years." He smiled. "Though I admit the waltz is my favorite. It allows conversation while dancing. I find that appealing."

"Of course you do. You never stop talking."

"I have much to say. After two hundred years of silence, I am making up for lost time."

Katie laughed. The heaviness of the afternoon lifted slightly.

"There is something I wanted to discuss with you," William said. His tone shifted. More serious. "About your accommodations."

"My accommodations?"

"You are currently housed in the family wing. Where you stayed during the courtship." He paused. "I would like to move you to the royal wing. Closer to me."

Katie's heart beat faster. "How close?"

"There is a consort's chamber. Adjacent to mine. Connected by a private door." He met her eyes. "I am not suggesting we share quarters.

I know you want to take things slowly. But I would feel better knowing you were nearby. Where I could reach you quickly if needed."

Katie considered this. The family wing was comfortable. Familiar. But it was also far from William's rooms. Far from the center of things.

"Can I see it?" she asked.

"Of course."

They walked through corridors Katie had not explored before.

The royal wing was different from the rest of the castle. More refined. Better maintained. The tapestries were newer. The floors were polished to a shine. Every detail spoke of care. Of attention.

William stopped before a door. Dark wood. Iron fittings. A crown carved into the surface.

"The consort's chamber," he said. "No one has used it since my mother died."

He opened the door.

Katie stepped inside and caught her breath.

The room was beautiful. High ceilings. Tall windows that looked out over the gardens. A fireplace large enough to stand in. Furniture that was old but elegant, all dark wood and soft fabrics.

And space. So much space. Her room in the family wing could have fit inside this one three times over.

"It has not been updated in some time," William said. "The furniture is original to my mother's era. But you may change anything you wish. Decorate it as you please. Make it yours."

Katie walked to the windows. The garden lights were on, and it looked breathtaking from this vantage point.

"Where is your room?" she asked.

"Through there." He pointed to a door on the far wall. "The connecting passage. You may lock it from your side. I would never enter without your permission."

Katie crossed to the door. Opened it. A short hallway led to another door, presumably to his chambers.

Private. But connected. Close enough to feel safe. Far enough to feel independent.

"Why would I bother decorating?" she asked.

William frowned. "I do not understand."

"Eventually, I'll be moving into your room. Right?" She turned to face him. "We're taking things slow, but we're not taking them forever. Why would I spend time making this space mine when I'll just be leaving it?"

Something shifted in William's expression. Surprise. And then a warmth that spread through the bond like sunlight.

"You are thinking ahead," he said.

"I'm thinking practically. You have a perfectly good bedroom through that door. It seems wasteful to maintain two."

"I appreciate the practicality." He moved toward her. Stopped a foot away. "But regardless of where you eventually sleep, this room will always be yours. A space that belongs to you alone. A place to escape when you need solitude."

"Or when I'm angry with you?"

"Especially when you are angry with me." He smiled. "I am told that will happen. Even the best relationships have conflict."

Katie laughed. "That's not how it works."

"What do you mean?"

"When you're in the doghouse, you don't get to stay in bed." She poked his chest. "You sleep on the couch."

William blinked. "I have to leave my own chambers?"

"If you've done something wrong? Yes. That's the rule."

"That seems unreasonable."

"That's marriage. Or whatever the vampire equivalent is."

William looked deeply concerned by this information. Katie found it hilarious.

"I have several couches," he said slowly. "I suppose I should determine which is most comfortable."

Katie laughed until her sides hurt. The bond hummed with shared amusement. With joy. With the simple, uncomplicated happiness of two people who had found each other against impossible odds.

"Come on," she said, wiping her eyes. "Show me where the first couch is. I want to make sure it's sufficiently uncomfortable."

"You are enjoying this far too much."

"I really am."

William sighed. But he was smiling.

26

The World Outside

The days blurred together.

Katie woke each afternoon to lists. Decisions. Questions that needed answers before the sun set. Julia had taken over her life with ruthless efficiency, and Katie was beginning to suspect the woman did not actually sleep.

"Flowers," Julia said on day three. "We need to finalize the arrangements. Roses are traditional, but lilies make a stronger statement. Or we could do both. What do you think?"

"Both sounds nice."

"Both it is." Julia made a note. "Now. The seating chart. We have three hundred confirmed guests and seventeen outstanding responses. I need to know your preferences for table arrangements."

"My preferences?"

"Who do you want near you? Who should be kept apart? There are factions among the vampire nobility. Placing the wrong people adjacent could cause incidents."

Katie stared at her. "I don't know any of these people."

"Then we will need to educate you. I have prepared dossiers."

Julia produced a stack of folders thick enough to stop a door. Katie's heart sank.

"All of them?"

"All of them. By next week, ideally."

Katie took the folders. They weighed approximately the same as her future.

The waltz lessons began on day five.

William had cleared a room in the east wing. Wooden floors. Mirrors along one wall. A gramophone in the corner that looked older than most countries but still played perfectly.

"The waltz is simple," William said. "Three beats. One two three. One two three. The pattern never changes."

"Easy for you to say. You've had centuries."

"And you have me." He extended his hand. "Come. I will show you."

She took his hand. He pulled her close. One hand at her waist. The other holding hers, raised to shoulder height.

"Follow my lead," he said. "Do not think. Just feel where I am going."

The music started. Something old. Classical. Katie did not recognize it, but her body seemed to respond anyway.

One two three. One two three.

She stepped on his foot immediately.

"Sorry."

"Do not apologize. Try again."

One two three. One two three.

She stumbled. Caught herself. Stepped on him again.

"This is impossible."

"This is learning." William smiled. "Again."

They practiced for an hour that first night. By the end, Katie could manage a full rotation without incident. It was not graceful. But it was something.

"Better," William said.

"That was terrible."

"That was progress. Tomorrow will be better still."

Tomorrow was better. And the day after. And the day after that.

By the end of the first week, Katie could waltz. Not beautifully. Not like someone who had spent centuries perfecting the art. But competently. Enough to survive a first dance without embarrassment.

"You are a quick learner," William said.

They were still in the practice room. The music had stopped. But neither of them had moved apart.

"I had a good teacher."

"You had a patient teacher. There is a difference."

Katie laughed. She was still in his arms. His hand still at her waist. His face closer than it had been a moment ago.

"William."

"Yes?"

"Are you going to kiss me?"

He went still. That absolute stillness that only vampires could manage.

"I would very much like to," he said carefully. "But you said you wanted to take things slowly."

"I did say that."

"And I meant it when I said your pace was our pace."

"You did."

"So unless you are telling me that you want me to kiss you, I will maintain appropriate distance and continue being patient."

Katie looked at him. At the face she had seen on television screens for half her life. At the man who had written her letters for eighteen years. At the king who had waited two centuries and would wait two more if she asked him to.

"I want you to kiss me," she said.

He kissed her.

It was gentle. Careful. The kiss of someone who had been waiting so long that he barely knew how to stop. His lips were warm against hers. Another change she was still getting used to.

The bond hummed between them. She could feel his joy. His relief. His overwhelming, desperate hope that this was real and he was not dreaming.

When he pulled back, his eyes were wet.

"I have imagined that for two hundred years," he said. "It was better than I imagined."

Katie laughed. Felt tears on her own cheeks. "You're very smooth for someone who's been waiting since before my country existed."

"I have had time to plan what I would say."

"And that's what you came up with?"

"I had several alternatives. Would you like to hear them?"

"Maybe later." She pulled him back down. "Kiss me again first."

He did.

The second week was harder.

Not because of the planning. Katie had found her rhythm with Julia. Decisions came easier now. She knew what she liked. What she wanted. What kind of Queen Consort she intended to be.

The hard part was everything else.

She had been living in a cocoon. The castle. The courtship. The bond. All of it had wrapped around her like silk, separating her from the world she had left behind.

On day ten, she decided to check her email.

It had been over a month. She had not thought about it. Had not missed the constant ping of notifications and messages. But now, settled in her new room with an afternoon to herself, she felt the pull of her old life.

She found her phone. Charged it. Watched the screen light up with weeks of accumulated chaos.

Two hundred and seventeen emails. Forty-three text messages. Nineteen missed calls.

She started with the texts.

Rachel: *OMG Katie is that you on TV?????*

Rachel: *Call me immediately*

Rachel: *Why aren't you answering*

Rachel: *I can't believe you didn't tell me*

Rachel: *Everyone is talking about you*

Rachel: *Are you seriously dating a vampire?*

Rachel: *THE vampire? The king one?*

Rachel: *Katie this is insane*

Rachel: *I thought we were friends*

Katie felt something cold settle in her stomach. She kept scrolling.

Messages from people she barely knew. Classmates who had never spoken to her. Distant relatives who had not called in years.

Some were curious. Some were excited. Some were cruel.

Always knew you were desperate

Gold digger

Vampire whore

Katie closed the texts. Opened her email. Found more of the same.

Requests for interviews. Media inquiries. Messages from strangers who had found her address somehow. And buried among them, emails from people she had considered friends.

I can't believe you would do this to your family

You always thought you were better than us

Enjoy your blood money

She should stop. She knew she should stop. But something made her keep going. Keep looking. Keep searching for something that would make sense of what she was seeing.

She opened a browser. Typed her name into the search bar.

The results were endless.

Mystery Pennsylvania teen snags vampire king

Who is Kathryn Parker? Everything we know about the new Queen Consort

From poverty to palace: The unbelievable story of William Stone's human mate

Katie clicked on a news video. A segment from an American network. The anchor was discussing the bonding announcement, showing the photographs from the castle.

"Opinions are divided on the match," the anchor said. "Some see it as a fairy tale. Others are more skeptical."

The screen cut to a street interview. A woman Katie did not recognize.

"I think it's beautiful. True love doesn't care about species."

Another interview. A man shaking his head.

"It's unnatural. Humans and vampires shouldn't mix. This is exactly what happens when we let them into our society."

Katie's chest tightened. She kept watching.

"We spoke with people who knew Kathryn Parker before her rise to royalty," the anchor said. "Their reactions may surprise you."

The screen changed. A face appeared. Familiar. Someone Katie had sat next to in class. Had eaten lunch with. Had considered, once, a friend.

Sarah Miller.

"Katie was always kind of desperate," Sarah said. She was sitting in what looked like her parents' living room. Looking directly at the camera. "Her family had nothing. Like, literally nothing. Her dad was always losing jobs. They could barely pay their bills."

Katie felt the words like blows.

"I'm not surprised she went for a vampire. A king, especially. I mean, think about how rich he must be." Sarah laughed. It was not a kind laugh. "She probably saw an opportunity and took it. Katie was always good at playing the victim. Making people feel sorry for her. I guess it finally paid off."

The segment ended. The anchor moved on to other news.

Katie sat frozen. The phone in her hands. The words echoing in her head.

Desperate. Nothing. Playing the victim.

She had thought Sarah was her friend. They had drifted apart after the job loss, but Katie had never thought she was hated. Had never imagined that someone she knew would go on television and say these things.

The bond flared.

She felt William's alarm before she heard his footsteps. Felt his concern like a hand on her shoulder. He was moving through the castle. Coming to her. Fast.

The door opened.

"Katie." He crossed the room in an instant. Knelt before her chair. "What happened? I felt..."

He saw the phone in her hands. The frozen image on the screen. Sarah's face, captured mid-sentence.

"Ah," he said quietly.

"I looked myself up." Katie's voice was flat. "I wanted to see what people were saying."

"And you found cruelty."

"I found the truth." She laughed. It sounded wrong. "About what people really think of me. About what my friends really think of me."

William took the phone from her hands. Set it aside. Took her hands in his instead.

"Listen to me," he said. "What you saw. What you read. It says nothing about you. It says everything about them."

"She was my friend."

"She was someone who knew you once. That is not the same thing." His grip tightened. "The moment you became visible, you became a target. Everyone who ever envied you. Everyone who ever resented you. Everyone who ever wanted something they did not have. They will use your rise to tear you down. It is what people do."

"Is that supposed to make me feel better?"

"No. It is supposed to prepare you." William's voice was gentle but firm. "This is your first lesson, Katie. The first of many. You cannot care what the public thinks of you personally. You cannot let their opinions shape how you see yourself."

"How am I supposed to do that?"

"By understanding what you are to them." He released one of her hands. Touched her chin. Lifted her face to meet his eyes. "You are a symbol now. Not a person. They do not see Katie Parker. They see the human who mated to the vampire king. They will project onto you whatever they wish to see."

"And if what they see is a gold digger from a broke family?"

"Then that is their failure of imagination. Not yours." William's expression was fierce. "You will always be the first person they diminish with their words. They will mock you. Question your motives. Assume the worst. But then. When they need help. When they need someone with power to listen. They will come to you. The same people who called you desperate will beg for your attention. The same voices that tore you down will ask you to lift them up."

Katie stared at him. "That's horrible."

"That is leadership. That is public life." He softened slightly. "I have lived it for decades. I know how much it costs. But I also know that the alternative is worse. Caring what they think will destroy you. It will eat you from the inside until there is nothing left."

"So I just... don't care?"

"You care about the people who matter. Your family. Your true friends. Me." He took her hands again. "You ignore the rest. You let their words pass through you like wind through leaves. You do the work that matters and you let the noise fade into background."

Katie thought about Sarah. About the texts and emails and comments from strangers. About the weight of a world that had decided who she was without ever knowing her.

"It's not fair," she said quietly.

"No. It is not." William pulled her forward. Wrapped his arms around her. Held her against his chest. "But you are not alone in it.

Whatever they say about you, they say about me as well. We carry this together."

Katie pressed her face into his shoulder. Let herself be held.

The bond hummed with his love. His concern. His fierce, protective anger at anyone who would hurt her.

She thought about the letters. Eighteen years of waiting. Two hundred years of solitude. He had endured far more than cruel comments from strangers. He had endured centuries of invisibility, and then years of fear and hatred when vampires revealed themselves.

If he could survive that, she could survive this.

"I'm sorry," she said into his shoulder.

"For what?"

"For falling apart. Over something so stupid."

"It is not stupid. It is painful. Pain deserves acknowledgment." He stroked her hair. "You are allowed to hurt, Katie. You are just not allowed to let the hurt define you."

She pulled back. Looked at him. At the ancient creature who had chosen her out of all the humans in the world.

"I love you," she said.

It was the first time she had said it. The words surprised her as much as they surprised him.

William went still. His eyes widened.

"What did you say?"

"I love you." The words came easier the second time. "I don't know when it happened. But I do. I love you. Can you feel it?"

The bond exploded with emotion. Joy so intense it was almost painful. Disbelief that slowly transformed into wonder.

"Say it again," he whispered.

Katie smiled through her tears.

"I love you, William."

He kissed her. Not gentle this time. Not careful. The kiss of someone who had waited two hundred years to hear those words and finally, finally had.

When they broke apart, they were both smiling.

"I love you too," he said. "I have loved you since before you were born. I will love you until long after the stars burn out."

"That's very dramatic."

"I am a very dramatic person. You will have to get used to it."

Katie laughed. The hurt was still there. The cruelty of the world had not vanished. But it felt smaller now. More manageable.

She was not alone.

She would never be alone again.

"Come on," she said. "Let's go practice the waltz. I need to step on your feet a few more times."

"I thought you had mastered it."

"I've mastered not falling down. Mastering grace will take at least another century."

"Fortunately," William said, pulling her to her feet, "we have time."

They walked out of the room together. Left the phone behind. Left the cruelty and the comments and the noise.

The world would still be there tomorrow. It would still be harsh and unfair and full of people who would never understand.

But so would he.

And that, Katie was learning, made all the difference.

27

The Ball

The gown was heavier than Katie expected.

She stood before the mirror in her chambers while three attendants made final adjustments. The dress was ivory silk, embroidered with silver thread that caught the candlelight. The neckline was modest. The sleeves were long. The skirt fell in layers that whispered when she moved.

Around her neck hung the pendant her mother had given her. The tiny crown. It seemed appropriate somehow. A piece of home against all this grandeur.

"Almost ready," one of the attendants said. "Just the hair."

Katie sat. Let them work. Watched in the mirror as her brown hair was twisted and pinned into something elegant. Something queenly.

She barely recognized herself.

A knock at the door.

"Katie?" Her mother's voice. "May we come in?"

Katie's heart lifted. "Yes. Please."

The door opened. Clara and Thomas stepped inside.

They had arrived that morning. Private flight, just as William had promised. Katie had wanted to meet them at the airfield, but Julia had forbidden it. Too much to do. Too many preparations.

But now they were here. Standing in her chambers. Looking at her like they had never seen her before.

"Oh, Katie." Clara's voice broke. "Look at you."

Thomas said nothing. His eyes were wet.

Katie stood. The gown rustled around her. She crossed to her parents and pulled them both into a hug, protocol be damned.

"I missed you," she said.

"We missed you too." Clara pulled back. Held Katie at arm's length. Studied her face. "You look different."

"The bond. It changes things."

"Not just that." Clara touched Katie's cheek. "You're glowing. Actually glowing."

"I'm happy, Mom." Katie smiled. "Genuinely, completely happy."

Clara's expression shifted. Wonder. Relief. A mother's joy at seeing her child flourish.

"I can tell," she said. "I can see it in every part of you."

Thomas found his voice. "The king. He's treating you well?"

"Better than well." Katie took her father's hand. "He loves me, Dad. Really loves me. And I love him."

Thomas nodded slowly. Whatever reservations he still carried seemed to ease.

"Then that's all that matters," he said.

The attendants cleared their throats politely. There was still work to be done.

"We should let you finish getting ready," Clara said. "We'll see you at the ball."

"You'll be there? In the hall?"

"Front row. The king arranged it." Clara smiled. "He said family should have the best seats."

They left. Katie returned to the mirror. Let the attendants finish their work.

The woman looking back at her was a stranger. Beautiful. Composed. Ready.

Katie took a deep breath.

It was time.

The great hall had been transformed.

Katie remembered it from her first tour. Vast and shadowed. Ancient stone and towering pillars. The two thrones watching from the raised platform.

Now it blazed with light.

Chandeliers hung from the ceiling, hundreds of candles burning in crystal holders. Flowers cascaded from every surface. Roses and lilies, just as she had chosen. The floor had been polished until it reflected like a mirror. An orchestra played softly in the corner. Music she did not recognize but that felt appropriate. Old and beautiful.

And the guests.

Three hundred of them, filling the hall like a sea of silk and jewels. Vampires in dark formal wear, their pale faces catching the candlelight. Humans in diplomatic attire, representatives of nations Katie had only read about.

They all turned when she appeared at the entrance.

Katie felt the weight of their attention like a physical force. Three hundred pairs of eyes. Three hundred judgments forming in an instant.

But then she felt something else.

William.

He was at the far end of the hall, standing before the thrones. He wore black, as always. But tonight his clothes were finer. More ornate. A king dressed for a celebration.

The bond hummed between them. She felt his pride. His love. His absolute certainty that she belonged here, beside him, no matter what anyone else thought.

She walked forward.

The crowd parted. Faces blurred past. She kept her eyes on William. Let his presence guide her through the sea of strangers.

Frederick stood beside the thrones. He stepped forward as Katie approached.

"Lords and ladies. Distinguished guests. Representatives of the human nations." His voice carried through the hall without effort. "I present to you Kathryn Parker, Queen Consort to His Majesty King William Stone."

Applause. Scattered at first, then growing. Katie climbed the steps to the platform. Took her place beside William.

He took her hand. Raised it to his lips.

"You are magnificent," he murmured. Low enough that only she could hear.

"I'm terrified."

"That too can be magnificent." He smiled. "Ready?"

"No."

"Good. Neither am I."

He turned to face the crowd. Katie turned with him.

"Thank you all for coming," William said. His voice filled the hall the way Frederick's had. The voice of a king addressing his people. "Tonight we celebrate not just a bond, but a future. A future where vampires and humans stand together. Where ancient traditions meet new possibilities."

He looked at Katie. His expression softened.

"I have waited two hundred years for this moment. For her. And I can tell you, without reservation, that every year of waiting was worth it."

More applause. Katie felt her face heat.

"Now." William's tone lightened. "Enough speeches. Let us dance."

The orchestra shifted. A waltz began.

William led her down from the platform and onto the floor. The crowd drew back, forming a circle around them.

"Remember," he said quietly. "One two three. One two three."

"If I step on you in front of three hundred people, I will never forgive myself."

"Then do not step on me."

"Very helpful."

"I try."

They danced.

Katie let the music carry her. Let William lead. Let the weeks of practice take over so her mind could quiet and her body could move.

One two three. One two three.

She did not step on him. Not once.

When the dance ended, the crowd applauded again. Other couples began to join them on the floor. The formal moment had passed. Now the celebration could truly begin.

"You did beautifully," William said.

"I did adequately."

"Adequate is beautiful when you are wearing that dress."

Katie laughed. The tension that had been coiling in her chest began to release.

"Come," William said. "There are people you should meet."

The next two hours were a blur of introductions.

Vampires first. Ancient creatures with names that sounded like history. Lords and ladies from every corner of the world.

"Lady Vivian you know," William said. "She has been with my family for three centuries."

Vivian inclined her head. Her expression was unreadable, but something like approval flickered in her eyes.

"Your Majesty," she said. "You dance better than I expected."

"Thank you. I think."

"It was a compliment. I do not give many."

They moved on. More vampires. More names.

Samuel appeared before them. The council member who had dismissed her at the dinner. Katie felt herself stiffen.

"Your Majesty." Samuel bowed deeply. To Katie, not to William. "I wish to offer my congratulations. And my apologies."

Katie glanced at William. He gave nothing away.

"Apologies for what?" she asked.

"For my behavior at the council dinner. It was inappropriate and disrespectful." Samuel's voice was stiff, but sincere. "I have served this crown for three centuries. I should know better than to dismiss someone based on age alone."

Katie considered him. The proud set of his shoulders. The effort it was costing him to say these words.

"Thank you," she said. "I appreciate that."

Samuel nodded. Moved away.

"That was gracious of you," William murmured.

"It was strategic. He's powerful, isn't he?"

"Very."

"Then I want him as an ally, not an enemy." Katie smiled slightly. "I'm learning."

William's pride swelled through the bond. "You certainly are."

The human dignitaries came next.

Ambassadors. Ministers. Representatives from a dozen nations. They approached with careful deference, unsure how to address a teenage girl who had become queen of an immortal species.

"Your Majesty." The American ambassador was a tall woman with sharp eyes. "On behalf of my government, congratulations."

"Thank you, Ambassador." Katie had practiced this. Julia had drilled her for hours. "I hope our nations can continue to work together under the Accord."

"As do we." The ambassador studied her. Whatever she saw seemed to satisfy her. "You're not what I expected."

"I get that a lot."

"I imagine you do." A small smile. "Good luck, Your Majesty. You're going to need it."

She moved on. More introductions followed.

Katie shook hands. Made small talk. Remembered names and titles and the proper forms of address. Her head spun, but she kept smiling. Kept performing.

This was her life now. This was what she had chosen.

She caught sight of her parents across the hall.

They stood near the edge of the crowd, watching her. Clara was crying. Thomas had his arm around her.

Katie excused herself from the conversation she was in. Made her way through the crowd.

"Mom. Dad."

Clara pulled her into a hug immediately. The embrace was fierce. Desperate.

"I'm so proud of you," Clara whispered. "So proud."

"You're doing wonderfully," Thomas added. "Like you were born for this."

"I was born for rural Pennsylvania and waitressing at the diner." Katie laughed. "This is all improvisation."

"Best kind of skill to have." Thomas smiled. His eyes were wet again. "Your grandmother would have loved this. Seeing you here. A queen."

Katie felt tears threaten. She blinked them back.

"I wish she could have been here."

"She is." Clara touched the pendant at Katie's throat. "Part of her is."

The music shifted. Another waltz began.

"May I?" a voice said behind her.

Katie turned. William stood there, hand extended.

"Your parents will forgive me if I steal you for another dance?"

"Go," Clara said. "Dance with your king."

The word still felt strange. But good strange.

Katie took William's hand. Let him lead her back onto the floor.

"Your parents seem happy," he said.

"They are. They're proud of me."

"As they should be." William pulled her closer than protocol probably allowed. "As am I."

They danced. Around them, the celebration continued. Music and laughter and the clink of crystal. Vampires and humans moving together in patterns as old as civilization.

"How do you feel?" William asked.

Katie considered the question.

She felt tired. Overwhelmed. Still slightly terrified.

But beneath all of that, she felt something else.

"I feel like I belong," she said.

William's expression shifted. Something raw and vulnerable crossed his features.

"You do belong," he said. "Here. With me. Always."

"Always is a long time."

"Not long enough." He smiled. "Not nearly long enough."

The waltz ended. Another began. They kept dancing.

The night stretched on. The candles burned lower. The crowd thinned as guests departed. But Katie and William stayed on the floor, moving together, lost in each other.

Eventually, the orchestra played its final song.

Katie looked around the great hall. At the flowers and the candles and the remnants of celebration. At the thrones on the platform, waiting for them.

"It's over," she said.

"The ball is over." William lifted her hand to his lips. "Everything else is just beginning."

They walked out of the great hall together. Past the servants cleaning up. Past Frederick, who nodded with something like approval. Past the last lingering guests.

The castle was quiet now. Peaceful.

Katie thought about the girl she had been a month ago. Waking up in Pennsylvania on her eighteenth birthday. Terrified of a knock at the door.

That girl was gone.

In her place stood a queen.

"William?" she said as they reached the royal wing.

"Yes?"

"Thank you."

"For what?"

She stopped. Turned to face him. "For giving me a life I never knew I wanted."

William cupped her face in his hands. His skin was warm against hers.

"Thank you for choosing it," he said. "For choosing me."

He kissed her. Soft and slow and full of promise.

When they broke apart, Katie was smiling.

"Take me to bed," she said.

William's eyes widened. "Katie..."

"Just to sleep. I'm exhausted." She laughed at his expression. "You didn't think I meant...?"

"I did not know what you meant. I was prepared for anything."

"Well, tonight I mean sleep. Tomorrow, we can discuss anything else."

He laughed. The sound echoed through the empty corridor.

"As my queen commands."

He took her hand. Led her to the royal chambers.

Tomorrow there would be more work. More learning. More challenges she could not yet imagine.

But tonight, there was just this.

Two people who had found each other against impossible odds.

A king and his queen.

A love that had waited two centuries to begin.

Katie fell asleep in William's arms, the bond humming between them, the future stretching out before them like an endless, starlit sky.

28

Taken

Katie needed clothes.

It was a simple problem. She had arrived at the castle with one suitcase. Her mother had packed practical things. Jeans. Sweaters. Comfortable shoes. Nothing that belonged in a queen's wardrobe.

The ball gown had been provided. So had a few formal pieces for meetings and dinners. But Katie's everyday clothes were running thin.

"I can have tailors come to you," William said. They were in his study, the evening stretching before them. "Designers. Entire shops, if you wish. You need not leave the castle."

"I've been in this castle for six weeks." Katie curled deeper into her chair. "I haven't left once. I'd like to see the town."

"The town is not safe."

"The town is full of humans going about their lives. It's perfectly safe."

"You are not just any human anymore."

"I know that." Katie met his eyes. "But I can't spend the rest of my very long life locked in a castle. I need to exist in the world sometimes. Starting with buying my own clothes."

William was quiet. She could feel his reluctance through the bond. His fear.

"The shops are only open during the day," she added. "You couldn't come anyway. Let me do this. Please."

He exhaled slowly. "You will take security."

"Of course."

"Human security during the day. Armed. Trained."

"Whatever you think is necessary."

William studied her. Whatever he saw in her face seemed to satisfy him, reluctantly.

"Very well," he said. "But if anything feels wrong. Anything at all. You come back immediately."

"I promise."

He pulled her close. Kissed her forehead.

"I worry," he said quietly.

"I know. That's one of the things I love about you."

The next morning, Katie left the castle for the first time since she had arrived.

The town was small. Quaint. Stone buildings and narrow streets. The kind of place that appeared on postcards and in travel magazines.

It was also full of cameras.

Katie noticed them immediately. Photographers on corners. Phones raised as she passed. The security team formed a loose perimeter around her, but they could not block every angle.

"Just ignore them," her lead guard said. His name was Grant. Former military. Calm in a way that suggested he had seen far worse than pa-parazzi. "They'll get bored eventually."

"Will they?"

"Probably not. But it sounds reassuring."

Katie laughed despite herself.

They made their way through the streets. People stopped and stared. Some waved. Some took pictures. A few approached, but the security team redirected them politely.

It was strange. Being recognized. Being watched. Katie had spent eighteen years being invisible. Now she could not take a step without someone noticing.

The boutique was small. Tucked down a side street. Grant had arranged it in advance. The shop would be closed to other customers for the duration of her visit.

"Take your time," he said. "We'll be right outside."

Katie stepped inside.

The shop was warm. Quiet. Racks of clothing lined the walls. A woman emerged from the back, middle-aged, nervous.

"Your Majesty. Welcome. I'm Helen. Please, let me know if you need anything."

"Thank you." Katie smiled, trying to put her at ease. "I'm just looking for everyday things. Nothing too formal."

"Of course. The fitting rooms are in the back. I'll bring you a selection."

Katie wandered through the racks. Touched fabrics. Pulled out pieces that caught her eye. It felt normal. Ordinary. Like being a regular person again, if only for an hour.

Helen brought armfuls of clothes. Dresses. Blouses. Trousers in cuts Katie had never tried. She carried them to the fitting room at the back of the shop.

The room was small. A mirror. A bench. A curtain for privacy.

Katie pulled it closed. Started to undress.

She was reaching for the first blouse when she heard it.

A sound behind her. Wrong. Out of place.

She turned.

The wall was moving.

Not the whole wall. A section of it. Swinging inward like a door she had not known was there.

A figure stepped through. Pale. Fast. Eyes she recognized.

Samuel.

Katie opened her mouth to scream.

His hand clamped over her face. Cold. Iron-strong. She could not make a sound.

"Quiet," he hissed. "This will be easier if you cooperate."

She did not cooperate.

She thrashed. Kicked. Clawed at his arm with her enhanced strength. But he was a vampire. Eight hundred years old. She was nothing to him.

He dragged her through the opening in the wall. Into darkness. Into a passage she could not see.

The last thing she heard was Helen's voice, calling from the front of the shop.

"Your Majesty? Is everything all right?"

Then the wall closed behind them.

And Katie was gone.

William woke screaming.

The bond exploded with terror. Pain. Desperation. Katie's fear flooded through him like ice water, drowning everything else.

He was on his feet before he was fully conscious. Running before he knew where he was going.

"Your Majesty!" Frederick's voice, somewhere behind him. "What is happening?"

"Katie." The word was a roar. "Someone has taken Katie."

He did not stop to explain. Did not stop for anything. He burst through the castle doors and into the daylight.

The sun hit him like a hammer. His skin began to burn immediately. He did not care. He could feel her. The direction. The distance. She was moving. Fast. Away from him.

"Guards!" Frederick's voice, growing distant. "All guards! Now!"

Vampires poured from the castle. They burned in the sunlight too. But they followed their king.

William ran.

He had never run this fast. Never pushed his body this hard. The bond pulled him forward like a rope around his chest. Every step brought more pain. The sun. The distance. The terror bleeding through from Katie.

She was hurt. He could feel it. Not badly. Not yet. But hurt.

He ran faster.

The landscape blurred around him. Hills. Forests. Villages that appeared and vanished in seconds. He crossed miles in minutes. Tens of miles in an hour.

The guards fell behind.

He heard them calling to him. Telling him to wait. To let them catch up. But he could not wait. Every second she was further away. Every second she was in danger.

Two hours. Three. Four.

His guards had stopped calling. They had exhausted their speed. Fallen back. He was alone now, running through the fading afternoon, powered by nothing but the bond.

Five hours.

And then, finally, she stopped moving.

William felt it like a physical shift. The desperate forward pull became a fixed point. She was there. Somewhere ahead. Still alive. Still afraid.

He pushed harder.

The cottage appeared out of nowhere. Run down. Abandoned. The kind of place that existed on the edges of forgotten roads.

William did not slow. He hit the door at full speed. It exploded inward.

Samuel stood in the center of the room.

He was alone. Katie lay on the floor behind him, bound, gagged, her eyes wide with terror and relief.

"Your Majesty." Samuel's voice was calm. Too calm. "I did not expect you so quickly."

William did not speak.

He crossed the room in a blur. His hand closed around Samuel's throat. Lifted him off the ground. Slammed him into the wall hard enough to crack the stone.

"You took her." The words were barely human. "You took my mate."

"I had to make you understand." Samuel's voice was strained. Choking. "The Echo Mark system. The Accord. All of it is a mistake. Vampires should not bind themselves to humans. We should not—"

William slammed him into the wall again. Harder.

"I do not care what you believe." His voice was ice. "You touched her. You hurt her. You will die for this."

Something flickered in Samuel's eyes. Confusion.

"How did you find us?" he gasped. "We traveled for hours. Crossed half the country. There is no way you should have—"

"The bond." William's grip tightened. "You have never mated. You do not understand what it means. I can feel her. Always. No matter where she is. No matter how far."

Samuel stared at him. For the first time, fear crept into his expression.

"I did not know," he whispered. "I did not understand."

"No. You did not."

The door burst open again. Guards poured in. Frederick at their head, burned and exhausted but still moving.

"Take him," William commanded.

They seized Samuel. Hauled him away. He did not resist.

William dropped to his knees beside Katie. His hands shook as he removed the gag. The ropes.

"Katie. Katie, look at me."

Her eyes found his. Tears streaked her face.

"William." Her voice was raw. "I knew you would come. I felt you. The whole time. Getting closer."

He pulled her into his arms. Held her against his chest. The bond sang with relief. With love. With the desperate, overwhelming gratitude of someone who had almost lost everything.

"I'm sorry," he said. "I'm so sorry. I should never have let you leave. I should have—"

"Don't." She pressed her face into his shoulder. "This isn't your fault. You saved me."

He held her tighter. Felt her pain through the bond. She was hurt. Bruises. Scrapes. Samuel had not been gentle in his transport.

"We need to get you home," he said. "You need a doctor."

"Where are we?"

William looked around. At the cottage. At the fading light outside. They had traveled far. Farther than he had realized.

"Far from home," he said. "Half the country, if Samuel was telling the truth."

He pulled out his phone. Made a call.

"I need a plane. Immediately. And a doctor on standby." He gave their location. Listened to the response. "One hour. Fine."

He hung up.

"An hour," he told Katie. "Then we're going home."

She nodded. She was shaking. Shock, probably. The aftermath of terror.

William wrapped his arms around her. Let her lean into him. Let the bond flow between them, carrying comfort and warmth and the absolute promise that he would never let this happen again.

They waited together in the ruined cottage as the sun set and the darkness gathered.

Frederick appeared in the doorway.

"Samuel is secured," he said. "He will face justice."

"He will face death." William's voice was flat. "This cannot stand."

Frederick nodded. He looked at Katie. Something like concern crossed his ancient face.

"The Queen Consort. Is she..."

"Hurt. Not badly." William stroked Katie's hair. "She is strong."

Frederick paused. "You ran for five hours, Your Majesty. At full speed. In sunlight. Your guards could not keep up. None of them."

"The bond."

"The bond." Frederick shook his head slowly. "I have served your family for three hundred years. I have never seen anything like what you did today."

William said nothing. He looked down at Katie, curled against his chest.

He would have run for fifty hours. Five hundred. However long it took.

That was what the bond meant. That was what love meant.

The plane arrived as promised. They lifted Katie carefully, carried her aboard. The doctor was already onboard, checking her injuries, confirming that nothing was broken.

Bruises. Scrapes. Exhaustion. Terror.

But alive. Whole. Safe.

They did not reach the castle until morning.

William carried Katie inside himself. Through the halls. Past the servants who stared. Up to the royal chambers.

He laid her in their bed. Pulled the covers over her. Sat beside her as her eyes fluttered closed.

"Stay with me," she murmured.

"Always."

"I mean it. Don't leave."

"I will never leave you." He took her hand. Held it tight. "Not for anything. Not ever."

She smiled. Small and tired and full of trust.

Then she slept.

William sat beside her and watched the sun rise through the windows. His skin still ached from the burns. His muscles screamed from the run. His heart had not stopped racing since he woke to her terror.

But she was here. She was safe. She was his.

And anyone who tried to take her again would learn exactly what happened to those who threatened a vampire's mate.

He would make sure of it.

29

Justice and Truth

Katie woke without pain.

She lay still for a moment, taking inventory. The bruises that had covered her arms were gone. The scrapes on her knees had healed. Even the deep ache in her muscles from being carried roughly across half the country had faded to nothing.

The bond. Still working. Still changing her.

She turned her head. William sat in a chair beside the bed, watching her. He looked better than he had last night. The burns on his skin had healed. The exhaustion in his eyes had eased.

"How do you feel?" he asked.

"Better. Much better." She pushed herself up against the pillows. "You?"

"Rested." He paused. "I need to do something today. Something you should know about."

Katie studied his face. The careful blankness of his expression.

"Samuel," she said.

"Yes."

"You're going to kill him."

It was not a question. She had known since the cottage. Since the moment William's hand had closed around Samuel's throat and he had spoken of death with absolute certainty.

"I have to." William's voice was quiet. "The law is clear. He took my mate. He hurt you. The punishment is death."

Katie thought about Samuel. About the fear in his eyes when he realized William had found them. About the eight hundred years of existence that were about to end.

"I'm not going to ask you to spare him," she said slowly. "I know you can't. I know the rules."

"But?"

"But I want to understand why." She met his eyes. "Not the law. Him. Why did he do it?"

William was silent for a moment.

"He believed the Accord was a mistake. That vampires should not bind themselves to humans. That the Echo Mark system weakens our kind by tying us to creatures who will always be lesser." His jaw tightened. "He thought if he took you. If he showed me what it felt like to lose a mate. I would understand. I would change."

"That's insane."

"That is ideology. It makes people do insane things." William stood. "I need to go. This cannot wait, it is not easy to hold a vampire."

Katie reached for his hand. Held it.

"I love you," she said.

"I love you too." He raised her hand to his lips. "I will be back soon."

Then he was gone.

The cells were beneath the castle.

William had not visited them in decades. There had been no need. Vampire justice was swift. Those who broke the laws were dealt with quickly. They did not linger in dungeons like characters in human stories.

Samuel was the exception.

He had been held for one day. Long enough for William to rest. Long enough for Katie to heal. Long enough for the reality of what he had done to settle into his ancient bones.

William descended the stairs alone. Frederick had offered to accompany him. He had refused. This was personal. This required no witnesses.

The cell was at the end of a long corridor. Iron bars. Stone walls. A single torch casting flickering shadows.

Samuel stood when William appeared. He looked diminished somehow. Smaller than he had seemed in the council chambers. Smaller than he had seemed in that cottage, with Katie bound at his feet.

"Your Majesty." His voice was hoarse. "I knew you would come."

William said nothing. He unlocked the cell door. Stepped inside.

"I want you to know," Samuel said quickly, "that I understand now. What I did was wrong. The bond. I did not realize how powerful it was. I did not understand."

"No. You did not."

"Please." The word cracked. "I have served this crown for three centuries. I have given everything to our people. One mistake. One terrible mistake. Does that erase all of it?"

William studied him. The fear in his eyes. The desperation in his voice. Eight hundred years of existence, begging for more.

"You took my mate," William said. "You hurt her. You terrorized her."

"I know. I know. And I am sorry. Truly sorry."

"Sorry is not enough."

"Then what is?" Samuel fell to his knees. "Tell me what to do. What penance to pay. I will do anything. Anything."

William looked down at him. At the creature who had once been powerful. Respected. A voice on the council that others listened to.

"You knew the law when you took her," William said. "You knew the punishment. You chose to act anyway."

"I thought I was saving our kind. I thought—"

"You thought wrong."

William moved.

It was fast. Faster than thought. His hands found Samuel's head and twisted. The sound was sharp. Final.

Samuel's body crumpled to the floor.

William stood over him for a long moment. Felt nothing. No satisfaction. No grief. Just the cold certainty that this was necessary. That the law existed for a reason. That anyone who touched his mate would meet the same end.

He turned and walked out of the cell.

Frederick waited at the top of the stairs.

"It is done?" he asked.

"It is done."

"And the body?"

"Handle it. I do not care how."

Frederick nodded. He did not ask questions. Did not offer commentary. He simply accepted and moved to carry out his king's wishes.

William walked back to the royal chambers. Back to Katie. Back to the only thing that mattered.

She was waiting for him when he returned.

She did not ask what had happened. She could feel it through the bond. The cold resolution. The grim necessity.

"Are you all right?" she asked.

"I am." William sat beside her on the bed. "I have killed before. This was not different."

"It feels different."

"Because it was for you." He took her hand. "I would kill a thousand Samuels if they threatened you. I would burn the world to keep you safe."

"That's terrifying."

"That is the truth."

They sat in silence for a while. The bond hummed between them. Comfort flowing both ways.

"I've been thinking," Katie said finally. "About why Samuel did what he did."

"Ideology. I told you."

"Not just that." She shifted to face him. "He didn't understand the bond. He didn't know you could track me. Didn't know how powerful the pull would be. He was genuinely shocked when you found us."

"He had never mated. He could not understand."

"Exactly." Katie paused. "But he's not the only one. How many vampires out there have never mated? How many of them don't understand what the bond really means?"

William considered this. "Most of them. Mated pairs are rare. The majority of our kind have only heard stories."

"And what stories do they hear? What do they actually know about the bond?"

"The basics. The mark. The pull. The connection."

"But not the details. Not what it actually feels like. Not how you can sense where I am. How you can feel my emotions. How you ran for five hours in sunlight because the bond wouldn't let you stop."

William was quiet. He understood what she was saying.

"We kept things private," Katie continued. "The details of our bond. What it means. How it works. We treated it as personal. Intimate. Not for public consumption."

"Because it is personal."

"But maybe that was a mistake." She squeezed his hand. "If Samuel had known. If he had truly understood what the bond meant. Would he have tried to take me?"

"Perhaps not."

"Then maybe others need to understand too. Not just vampires. Humans. Everyone." Katie met his eyes. "Maybe we need to tell them."

William thought about it. About the privacy he had guarded so carefully. About the intimate details of their connection that he had shared with no one.

But Katie was right. Ignorance had nearly cost him everything. If others understood the bond. If they knew what it truly meant to threaten a vampire's mate. Perhaps they would think twice.

"An interview," he said slowly. "We could do an interview. Explain the bond publicly."

"Yes. Talk about what happened. Why you were able to find me. What the connection actually means."

"It would require sharing things I have never shared."

"I know." Katie's voice was gentle. "But it might prevent this from happening again. To us. To other mated pairs."

William nodded slowly. The decision settled into place.

"Very well," he said. "We will tell them. All of it."

The interview was arranged for the following week.

They chose a neutral location. A broadcast studio in Edinburgh. Human crew, but vampire security. The interviewer was a woman named Melissa Anderson, respected by both species for her fairness.

Katie dressed carefully. Simple clothes. Nothing too formal. She wanted to seem approachable. Human. Someone the audience could relate to.

William wore his usual black. He did not change for anyone.

The studio was bright. Hot under the lights. Cameras positioned at multiple angles. Katie had done nothing like this before. Her heart raced.

William took her hand. Squeezed.

"Together," he said quietly.

"Together," she agreed.

The interview began.

"Your Majesties," Melissa said. "Thank you for agreeing to speak with us. I understand you have something important to share."

"We do." William's voice was calm. Controlled. The voice of a king addressing his people. "Recent events have made us realize that there is much the world does not understand about the mate bond. We wish to correct that."

"You're referring to the kidnapping attempt."

"Yes. Queen Consort Katie was taken from a shop in town. Held for hours. Transported across the country by a vampire who believed he could use her against me."

"Samuel Ward. A member of your own council."

"Former member." William's voice hardened slightly. "He has been dealt with according to our laws."

Melissa nodded. She did not press for details. Everyone knew what vampire justice meant.

"Tell us about the bond," she said. "What does it actually mean to be mated?"

William glanced at Katie. She nodded.

"The Echo Mark identifies a potential match," William said. "But the mark is only the beginning. When a vampire meets their true mate, there is a pull. A physical sensation. An awareness of the other person that goes beyond normal perception."

"Can you describe it?"

"I can feel Katie. Always. The direction she is in. The rough distance between us." He paused. "I can also feel her emotions. Her joy. Her fear. Her pain. When Samuel took her, I felt her terror like it was my own. I woke from sleep screaming because the bond would not let me rest while she suffered."

The studio was silent. Even the crew had stopped moving.

"And when you pursued them," Melissa said carefully. "We've heard reports that you ran for five hours. In daylight. That your guards could not keep up."

"That is correct."

"How is that possible? Sunlight burns vampires."

"It does. I burned for every moment of those five hours." William's voice was matter-of-fact. "But the bond is stronger than pain. Stronger than exhaustion. Stronger than anything I have ever experienced. Katie was in danger. Nothing else mattered."

Katie spoke for the first time. "I could feel him coming. The whole time I was held, I could feel him getting closer. It was the only thing that kept me from losing hope."

"You share the connection as well?"

"Yes. Not as strongly as William. I'm human. But I know when he's near. I know when he's happy or worried or angry." She paused. "And I knew, even when Samuel had me, that William would find me. The bond told me he was coming."

Melissa leaned forward. "Samuel Ward was eight hundred years old. A senior member of the vampire council. What made him think he could succeed?"

"Ignorance." William's voice was cold. "He had never mated. He did not understand what the bond truly meant. He thought distance would protect him. He thought I would not be able to find her." A pause. "He was wrong."

"And that's why you're here today. To explain the bond. To prevent this kind of ignorance."

"Yes." Katie took over. "We kept the details of our bond private because they felt personal. Intimate. But that privacy came at a cost. Samuel acted out of ignorance. Others might too. We want everyone to understand what they're dealing with."

"So let me be clear." Melissa looked directly at the camera. "If someone threatens the mate of a vampire. If they try to take them. To hurt them. What happens?"

William answered. His voice carried the weight of two hundred years and the authority of a king.

"They die. Without exception. Without mercy." He paused. "A vampire will cross any distance. Endure any pain. Break any obstacle. There is no hiding. No escaping. The bond will lead us to our mate, and we will destroy anyone who stands in the way."

The words hung in the air.

"That sounds like a warning," Melissa said.

"It is." William looked at the camera. "To anyone who might consider what Samuel considered. To anyone who thinks threatening a vampire's mate is a viable strategy. You will fail. You will be found. And you will face justice."

He let the silence stretch.

"But it is also an invitation," he continued. "To understand. The mate bond is not a weakness. It is a strength. It binds us together. Makes us better. Gives us something worth protecting." He glanced at Katie. "I would not trade it for anything."

Katie smiled. Took his hand.

"Neither would I," she said.

The interview aired that night.

By morning, it had been viewed by millions. Human and vampire alike. The footage of William describing his five-hour run through daylight spread across every platform. The warning echoed through every discussion.

Katie watched the reactions from the safety of the castle. Some were supportive. Some were frightened. Some called them monsters.

But all of them understood now.

The bond was real. The bond was powerful. And anyone who threatened it did so at their own peril.

"Do you think it will help?" she asked William.

"I think it will make people think twice." He pulled her close. "And that is enough."

Katie leaned into him. Let the bond hum between them.

They had shared their truth with the world. Opened themselves up. Made themselves vulnerable.

But they had also made themselves clear.

No one would take her again.

And if they tried, they would learn exactly what William Stone was capable of.

The hard way.

30

Forever Begins

The gardens were different tonight.

Katie noticed it the moment William led her outside. More lights than usual. Strings of them woven through every hedge and trellis. Lanterns hanging from posts she had not seen before. The whole space glowed like something from a dream.

"What is this?" she asked.

William said nothing. He led her to the center of the garden, to a clearing she had walked through a dozen times before. But tonight it was transformed. A circle of candles. Flowers scattered across the grass. The fountain that had not worked for decades now bubbled gently, catching the light.

"William."

He turned to face her. His expression was different. Nervous in a way she had never seen from him. Nervous in a way she had not known a two-hundred-year-old vampire king could be.

"I have something to ask you," he said.

Katie's heart began to pound.

"Vampires do not marry," William continued. "The bond is our commitment. Our ceremony. It is considered enough."

"I know."

"But you are not just a vampire's mate. You are human. You come from a world where marriage means something. Where a ring and a vow carry weight." He paused. "And your family. Your parents. They deserve to see their daughter married. Properly. In a way they understand."

Katie felt tears prick her eyes. "William."

He reached into his pocket. Pulled out a small box. Dark velvet. Old.

"This belonged to my mother," he said. "My father gave it to her the day they decided to spend their lives together. She wore it for fifty-five years." He opened the box.

The ring was beautiful. Simple. A single stone set in silver, worn smooth by decades of wear. It glowed in the candlelight like a captured star.

"Kathryn Parker." William's voice was steady now. Certain. "You have given me more than I ever dared to hope for. You have chosen me. Bonded with me. Stood beside me through challenges that would have broken anyone else."

He lowered himself to one knee.

"I am asking you to marry me. Not because the bond requires it. Not because tradition demands it. But because I want the world to know, in every way possible, that you are mine and I am yours." He looked up at her. "Will you be my wife?"

Katie was crying. She had not noticed when she started. The tears simply fell, warm against her cheeks.

"Yes," she whispered.

Then, stronger: "Yes. Of course yes."

William slid the ring onto her finger. It fit perfectly. As if it had been waiting for her all along.

He stood. Pulled her into his arms. Kissed her with all the passion of two hundred years of waiting and the promise of centuries more.

When they broke apart, he was smiling. That rare, genuine smile that transformed his whole face.

"I have another question," he said.

"Another one?"

"Would it be too forward to ask if we might do this tonight?"

Katie stared at him. "Tonight? William, I have nothing. No dress. No guests. No time to prepare anything."

"I have taken care of it all." His smile widened. "In hope."

"Taken care of what?"

"Everything. The dress. The venue. The officiant." He gestured to the transformed garden around them. "This is not just a proposal, Katie. This is preparation."

She looked around. At the candles. The flowers. The lights that had multiplied since her last visit.

"You planned this."

"I hoped. I planned in case the hope was answered."

Katie laughed. It was too much. Too perfect. Too overwhelming.

"But my parents," she said. "They should be here. They deserve to see this."

"They are here."

Katie froze. "What?"

"I flew them in yesterday. They have been waiting in the castle since this morning." William's expression softened. "I asked your father for his blessing. He gave it. Reluctantly at first. Then with something that looked almost like approval."

"They're here. Right now."

"Right now. Waiting to watch their daughter get married."

Katie pressed her hand to her mouth. The tears came harder now.

"You did all this for me."

"I would do anything for you." William cupped her face in his hands. "You are my mate. My queen. And after tonight, my wife. I wanted to give you everything. Every tradition. Every moment. Every memory you deserve."

Katie kissed him. Fierce and grateful and full of love.

"Take me to get ready," she said. "Before I change my mind."

"You would never change your mind."

"No. But I might decide we should just elope instead."

"That would be unfortunate. I have already paid for the flowers."

She laughed. Let him lead her back inside. Let the reality of what was happening settle into her bones.

She was getting married. Tonight. To a vampire king who had waited two centuries and had somehow managed to surprise her.

The dress was waiting in her chambers.

It hung in the center of the room, lit by candles, looking like something from a fairy tale. Ivory silk. Delicate lace. A train that would flow behind her like water.

"William chose it," one of the attendants said. "He said it reminded him of starlight."

Katie touched the fabric. Soft. Weightless. Perfect.

Her mother burst through the door.

"Katie!" Clara crossed the room and pulled her into a hug. "I can't believe this. I can't believe he did all this."

"Neither can I."

"Your father is with the king. Pretending to be stern and protective. I don't think William is fooled."

Katie laughed. "Probably not."

"Let me look at you." Clara pulled back. Studied her daughter's face. "You're glowing again. More than before."

"I'm happy, Mom. Completely, ridiculously happy."

"I can see that." Clara's eyes filled with tears. "My baby. Getting married."

"To a vampire king."

"To someone who loves you. That's all that matters."

The attendants moved around them. Preparing. Primping. Working their quiet magic.

Katie sat before the mirror as they styled her hair. Watched her mother fuss with the dress. Let herself be pampered in a way she had never experienced before.

This was real. This was happening.

In an hour, she would be a wife.

The garden was filled with people.

Not many. Fewer than thirty. But the ones who mattered.

Her parents stood at the front, Clara already crying, Thomas looking proud and slightly terrified. Frederick was there, ancient and formal, serving as William's witness. Julia had somehow managed to make herself indispensable and stood near the back, clipboard in hand.

And William.

He stood beneath an arch of flowers, wearing black as always, but finer than she had ever seen. His eyes found hers the moment she appeared at the end of the aisle.

The bond flooded with emotion. His love. His wonder. His absolute disbelief that this moment had finally arrived.

Katie walked toward him.

The lights glowed around her. The fountain bubbled softly. Music played from somewhere she could not see. Everything was soft and golden and perfect.

She reached him. Took his hands.

"You look like starlight," he whispered.

"You look like you're about to cry."

"I might. Do not tell Frederick."

The officiant stepped forward. An elderly vampire Katie did not recognize. His voice carried clearly through the garden.

"We are gathered here to witness the marriage of King William Stone and Kathryn Parker. This union is unusual in our world. Vampires do not traditionally marry. But love has never cared for tradition, and these two have chosen to honor both worlds they belong to."

Katie squeezed William's hands. He squeezed back.

"William. Your vows."

William took a breath. For a moment, he looked almost human. Young and nervous and full of hope.

"Katie. I have lived for two hundred years. I have seen empires rise and fall. I have watched the world change in ways I never imagined. But nothing in all those years has meant as much to me as you."

His voice steadied.

"I vow to protect you. To cherish you. To stand beside you through whatever challenges we face. I vow to be patient when you need patience. To be strong when you need strength. To be soft when you need softness." He paused. "I vow to love you for as long as I exist. And when the stars burn out and the universe goes dark, my last thought will still be of you."

Katie was crying again. She did not care.

"Katie. Your vows."

She had not prepared anything. Had not known she would need to. But the words came anyway, rising from somewhere deep inside.

"William. A few short months ago, I was a girl from Pennsylvania who had never been anywhere or done anything. I was afraid of the future. Afraid of the world. Afraid of becoming someone I didn't recognize."

She looked into his eyes. Dark and ancient and full of love.

"You changed that. Not by making me less afraid. But by showing me that fear was just the beginning. That on the other side of it was something worth having." She squeezed his hands. "I vow to be your partner. Your equal. Your home. I vow to argue with you when you're wrong and support you when you're right. I vow to throw cushions at you when you're being pretentious and kiss you when you make me laugh."

A ripple of laughter moved through the small crowd.

"I vow to love you," Katie continued. "For as long as this enhanced, ridiculous, impossible life of mine lasts. And if you're right about the universe going dark, I'll be right there beside you. Probably still arguing about whether Scottish rain has more character than American rain."

William laughed. A real laugh. The kind she loved.

"By the power vested in me," the officiant said, "I pronounce you husband and wife. You may kiss your bride."

William pulled her close. Kissed her deeply. The crowd applauded.

When they broke apart, Katie was smiling so wide her face hurt.

"Hello, husband," she said.

"Hello, wife." William's eyes were wet. He did not try to hide it. "I have been waiting my whole life to say that."

"Was it worth the wait?"

"Every single moment."

The reception was intimate.

A long table in the small dining room. Candles everywhere. Food that appeared in courses, each one more beautiful than the last.

Katie sat beside William and watched her parents laugh with Frederick. Watched vampires and humans mingle like it was the most natural thing in the world. Watched her life knit itself together into something she had never imagined.

Her mother found her during a quiet moment.

"I'm so proud of you," Clara said. "Everything you've become."

"I'm still me, Mom."

"I know. That's why I'm proud." Clara kissed her forehead. "Be happy, Katie. That's all I've ever wanted for you."

"I am. I really am."

The evening wound down slowly. Guests departed. Congratulations were offered. Eventually, only the family remained.

Katie hugged her parents goodbye. They would stay in the castle tonight. Return home tomorrow. But this moment was for her and William.

"Thank you," Katie whispered to her father. "For giving your blessing."

Thomas held her tight. "He asked me a week ago. Called me on the phone like a nervous teenager." He pulled back. Smiled. "Any man who's that scared of asking permission is the right man."

Katie laughed. Kissed his cheek.

Then William's hand was in hers, and they were walking through the castle together. Down corridors she knew by heart now. Up stairs she had climbed a hundred times.

To their chambers.

He opened the door. Led her inside.

The room was filled with candles. Rose petals scattered across the floor. Their bed waited, soft and warm and full of promise.

Katie turned to face him.

Her husband. Her king. Her mate.

"William."

"Yes?"

She reached up. Touched his face. Let her fingers trace the lines she had memorized. The features she would know for centuries to come.

"Make love to me, my mate."

William's eyes darkened. His hands found her waist. Drew her close.

"As my wife commands," he whispered.

He kissed her.

And the rest of the world disappeared.

9 781764 446235